GRIM TALES

THE EAST MIDLANDS

Edited by Jenni Bannister

First published in Great Britain in 2015 by:

 Young Writers

Remus House
Coltsfoot Drive
Peterborough
PE2 9BF
Telephone: 01733 890066
Website: www.youngwriters.co.uk

Printed and bound in the UK by BookPrintingUK
Website: www.bookprintinguk.com

FOREWORD

Welcome, Reader!

For Young Writers' latest competition, Grim Tales, we gave secondary school pupils nationwide the tricky task of writing a story with a beginning, middle and an end in just 100 words. They could either write a completely original tale or add a twist to a well-loved classic. They rose to the challenge magnificently!

We chose stories for publication based on style, expression, imagination and technical skill. The result is this entertaining collection full of diverse and imaginative mini sagas, which is also a delightful keepsake to look back on in years to come.

Here at Young Writers our aim is to encourage creativity in young adults and to inspire a love of the written word, so it's great to get such an amazing response, with some absolutely fantastic stories. This made it a tough challenge to pick the winners, so well done to Natasha Burton who has been chosen as the best author in this anthology.

I'd like to congratulate all the young authors in Grim Tales – The East Midlands – I hope this inspires them to continue with their creative writing. And who knows, maybe we'll be seeing their names on the best seller lists in the future...

Jenni Bannister

Editorial Manager

CONTENTS

THE
MINI SAGAS

BETTER THAN PORRIDGE

There she was - the infamous outlaw. Her shimmering hair glistening in the sunlight... disgusting. A tartan dress covering her adolescent figure and knee-high leather boots, ripped and torn. Her slender body made me sick. She took the bait. Was she resisting? No; the poison had done its job. Father said that one spoonful would send her down within ten seconds. On the floor... we pounced. I hacked off her limbs; took out the organs and cooked it in a monstrous stew. One hour later and our taste buds were partying. Goldilocks tastes much better than boring, bland, old porridge.

HARRY REDFERN (14)
Abington Academy & Arts College, Wigston

THE LITTLE GIRL WITH THE GOLDEN HAIR

I was all alone in the little, thatched cottage, wrapped up cosily in bed. Suddenly, I heard the front door creak open and the pitter-patter of unfamiliar feet scurry across the kitchen. There was a slurping sound; my porridge had been consumed. Next there was a loud snap and a harsh cry from the living room. Slowly they began to make their way towards my bedroom door. My heart began to beat so fast that it was almost audible. The door swung open, there stood a little girl with long golden locks of hair. That was it, I fled!

PRIYA BASSI (14)
Abington Academy & Arts College, Wigston

THE COTTAGE

The young girl skipped through the forest with her long, blonde hair trailing behind her. She came across a nice little cottage. *What's wrong with taking a look inside?* she thought. Inside the cottage there was a unique smell and it didn't look as nice as the outside. There was no furniture, apart from three dog beds, three bowls and three bones. Everything came in three sizes: small, medium and large. She looked in the corner where the unique smell was coming from and saw a pile of red paint. Well, that's what she thought. 'Wolves!' she screamed - then silence...

AMY GROVE (17)
Chesterfield College, Chesterfield

TILL DEATH US DO PART

There was a deafening thud as he hit the ground. Strange concept, death. In one moment there was a man with an address, a phone number and a driver's licence and then next all that remained was an object. An object as material and inhuman as a brick or a chair. These were the thoughts that possessed Keyoanna as her frightened, motionless body was rocked back and forth by the wind at the top of the steeple. She stared down at her husband, Arnold's corpse, the blood pooling around it from the crack in the back of his skull.

JOHN MORGAN REANEY (17)
Chesterfield College, Chesterfield

THE LITTLE NUISANCE

High in the sky a giant did stand up upon a beanstalk. Up went a boy called David, though he did not come back; by the giant he was caught. He tried to hide, oh he tried and tried, but it was no good as in the end there was nowhere to hide. With a fee, a fi, a fo and a fum, he found the little boy. Scared, the poor little boy pulled out his slingshot, he pulled back and shot, but defeat the giant it did not. The giant crushed him under his foot!

BRADY MOODY (17)
Chesterfield College, Chesterfield

THE BIRTH OF THE WOLF

The forest was bathed in blood and moonlight. A man stood in a clearing, drenched in red and glowing silver. A change overtook him. Bones broke and lengthened, muscles tore and regrew stronger; his raven hair grew and grew, until it spread across his face, down his shoulders and back. It spread down his chest and stomach and continued across his body. His jaw broke and changed shape, jutting forward like a muzzle; his teeth grew long and sharp, made to rend flesh. Claws erupted at the end of his fingers and toes. The Wolf was born that night. Beware!

RYAN SPENCER (18)
Chesterfield College, Chesterfield

MY NIGHTMARE

We were going to the beach. It was my worst nightmare. It doesn't sound bad, but it is. I hate the beach; sand in my eyes, salt giving me a rash and the sun burning my face till I look like a tomato. There's also the dreaded seagulls that swoop down at you when you least expect it. My family say I'm over-reacting, they say the beach is a place to relax. But I think it's a place that can haunt your dreams forever. I hoped this time would be better, but no! It was the worst day ever... ever!

CATHERINE POTTER (11)
Dagfa School, Nottingham

A HOUSE WITH A PAST

1933, it was 3am. I didn't want to go to sleep, this house - it scared me! It was old and creepy. I saw a flash, I jumped up, I tried to get out! Locked!
'It's OK, we're safe in here!' whispered a voice.
A little girl, with glowing white eyes and a bloodstained maid's dress, smiled menacingly at me. Another appeared and another and another, all crowding round me.
'Goodnight,' they whispered. Then... blackout.
2008: 'So glad you liked this house! All the rumours of it being haunted are of course, fake!' the estate agent smilingly told the family...

ELLA KUCUKDURGUT (11)
Dagfa School, Nottingham

Dave

Meet Dave, he's a fish. He's swimming (well, sort of), underwater. Dave's happy. Dave's previous owners freed him from the round, glass thing. Dave has even met Julie, a lobster, and Alan, a trout. They didn't like Dave. They didn't like blobfish. Dave was alone, he did have one friend though, Colin, the majestic swimming flea. People were giving Colin funny looks at the local swimming pool, so he decided to join Dave. Without warning the water turned ice-cold, Dave and Colin's stomachs dropped. A waterfall. It was the best moment of their lives. They continued their epic journey.

Joella Hinsley (11)
Dagfa School, Nottingham

Rapunzel?

I've been in this tower for over 15 years, living in fear, hiding from the world. There's not one day goes by that I don't wonder why I'm here and what I've done. Living as a slave, subservient to this abusive monster. Hit, smacked, punched and kicked just for speaking to her. I ask myself every day, 'Why me?'
I know that this person isn't my mother, but who is she? Why does she treat me like this and most of all, how do I escape? I hear a door open - 'Come on, we're going to be late for school!'

Hana Hussain (13)
Dagfa School, Nottingham

Extreme RKO

The ground around was rising up as I fell, but I was safe. I had the parachute strapped to my back and my goggles were stuck firmly to my greasy face. New York was right below me; the Empire State Building was rising up to meet me. I felt as light as air and as fast as a rocket. Then, out of the corner of my eye, I saw a man on the edge of the Empire State Building and an idea flew through my mind. RKO, out of nowhere - damn! The Internet had blown up!

PETER DALY (13)
Dagfa School, Nottingham

Maths Test

Come on, I can do this, it's not that hard. Cram, cram, cram, I have to absorb this information. Allied angles, alternate angles and... it's no use, I'll never be able to remember this. I'm dead, unless...
Later: 'Dear, most honourable headmaster, I've noticed that we haven't had a fire drill for a while and I think that we should keep up with the school safety standards. So please, could we have a fire drill at precisely 9 o'clock this morning? Yours sincerely, Matt'.
Meanwhile: 'You have 40 minutes to complete this test.'
Maybe I should've included a bribe!

SEAN MORRISSEY-RALEVIC (11)
Dagfa School, Nottingham

WITCH DISCRIMINATION

Ripping down tiles, breaking walls, smashing windows, damaging my property. A pair of youths, a pair of vandals, juvenile delinquents. They swing open the door, striding in like they own the place. They stare at me, open-mouthed. I'm ugly and I wear black. They judge me by my appearance and call me evil witch. Being polite, I show them round my house. They stare at cobwebs, rats, terrified of a lack of cleaning. I lead them into the kitchen, they see the oven lying open. They grab me and throw me in; murdering an old lady because she's ugly.

ADAM TING (12)
Dagfa School, Nottingham

ONE PIZZA IN TWENTY YEARS

I'm next to the pizza oven and I'm watching Kev put the pizza in it.
'Look! Kev's fallen in the oven!'
Damn, I was looking forward to that pizza. I'll go to the shops. 'One good pizza please.'
'Barbara! It's my coffee break,' said the young lady behind the till.
'Wow! You're fat! You're supposed to eat the food inside the fridge - not the fridge itself.'
Now I'm outside the shop - my rudeness got me ejected. I'll go home. The police came and arrested me for Kev's murder...
20th year in prison, it's pizza on the menu today. Yes, finally!

ADAM PRICE (12)
Dagfa School, Nottingham

Where Is My Sister?

It was a bright, sunny day with birds and an ice cream truck on the beach. I know that sounds nice and not scary at all; for me, it was my worst nightmare! I was screaming. I'd lost my sister. I couldn't find her because we were playing a game of hide-and-seek...
I asked everyone, 'Where's Skylar?'
Everyone replied, 'Have you checked on the beach?'
I would reply, 'Yes.'
I finally could hardly breathe, I'd been running for ages. Then, as I was walking, it hit me, what about the stairs? Then I found Skylar - my teddy!

Jessica Horan (11)
Dagfa School, Nottingham

Oh No!

In the future, the sea flooded the land. The people were all dead, just some super-people were still alive. These important people were hiding under the sea, but there wasn't much oxygen, so they died. The ordinaries were all dead because they were too old. There was one last person on Earth, his boat was broken but he was lucky, because he found an island in the sea. There was an old house with food and drink inside. He was tired and rested in the house. Then someone knocked on the door. 'Who's that?' he asked...

Kailai He (12)
Dagfa School, Nottingham

DREAMING?

I see a person in the dark - scary, black eyes, long blonde hair, standing looking at me. I look away and try to forget the terrifying face. Actually, I'm not sure if it is a person... I had that frightening dream and wake up quickly. I look out of the window to try to see the person, (if it was a person). Was it a dream? Yes? No? Maybe, just maybe. I blink again. No! The mysterious person is still out there. If it is a person out there. In one more blink of an eye, the face disappears.

SUNNIVA SULEN (12)
Dagfa School, Nottingham

GET OUT! GET AWAY!

Jimmy Crystal had just opened up a bar of his own. It's what he had always dreamed of. It was Thursday the 13th.
'Jimmy Crystal,' Billy started, 'do you know about the legend of this bar's stalker?'
'No. Why?'
'The legend is that it comes out at night on Thursday the 13th, today,' Billy said. 'If he sees you, you'll hear a voice in your head, which says, 'Get out, Get away'. It's a monster.'
That night Jimmy was cleaning up in the bar. He heard footsteps (not his). Then he heard a voice in his head. 'Get out, get away!'

RUARAIDH JAMES THOMSON (12)
Dagfa School, Nottingham

Nan

Just got back to school after the Christmas holidays. On that Monday my nan said, 'I love you,' as usual.
I replied, 'I love you too.'
Back at the house, I turned on the TV. I was eating pizza. My mum and nan were eating dreadful soup. My nan went upstairs, but Mum forgot to turn off the heating.
Minutes later Mum came rushing to tell me - 'Your nan's shaking!'
I went in and was holding her hand. Well, I hate to say what happened, but an aneurysm caused it... In memory of Doreen Chowdhury. I hated that day!

OLIVER CHOWDHURY (11)
Dagfa School, Nottingham

The Huntsman

Click! The last round was secured in the huntsman's rifle clip. When the huntsman left the house, he set off towards the wood to the right of his house. He had hunted there for years as gamekeeper. He was hired to keep down the deer population; to drive away the wolves that had moved in. Earlier that morning, he had heard them take down a deer, so he knew where they were. When the huntsman approached the area, he heard a sudden snarl from behind him and then more, from all around him. He was surrounded - he was dead.

WILL BRAMALL-SHAW (13)
Hope Valley College, Hope Valley

DAY IS DARK

I was outside, just enjoying my afternoon. But suddenly it turned dark, clouds covering the sun, the day turned to night, rain and lightning pouring down heavily. As it was pitch-black I panicked. How could I find my way out of this dead, dark space? But then I saw a flicker of light in the distance. I followed it. I stopped running towards it when I saw a shadow. So big.

I started to walk back, a man came round the corner, but he didn't look very well. He came closer and closer, he clenched his fist - I screamed...

SOFIA ELLIOTT (12)
Hope Valley College, Hope Valley

THE BODY

Jack stepped into the glade, only to see a pale body lying on the ground. The body looked like it had been strangled! Jack froze, wondering if the killer was still there. *Snap!* A twig broke behind Jack. Now petrified, Jack spun round, to see a hooded man running at him with his hands held up, ready to strangle him. Stumbling backward, Jack tripped over the body. The man chuckled. He said, 'Enjoy your last breath.' Jack knew this was the end.

WILL MARSDEN (12)
Hope Valley College, Hope Valley

The Last Man

I was asleep in my warm, comforting bed until there was a noise. A loud noise, a noise that nearly made my ears bleed. I woke up like I had just been dead. I went towards the window and looked outside. No one was there, It felt a bit strange. There's normally people outside looking around the busy streets of London. I put my clothes on and went outside. I walked to the local market, which was normally packed by now. Nobody - no one was there. My heart was racing. 'What should I do?'

James Asquith (13)
Hope Valley College, Hope Valley

The Pier

Hi, I'm Isla and this is my story. My friend went on this dating site and she booked a date with this guy called Thomas. They arranged to meet by the pier. So I tagged along with her, knowing there was no one around, just them. But I hid where they couldn't see me.
First they got ice cream and then they were standing on the pier. Next thing I knew, Bella was dead on the rocks down in the sea. I got a knife, as keen-edged as a pinprick. He collapsed and I laughed.

Ella Perry (12)
Hope Valley College, Hope Valley

IT

There it lay. Twisting and turning, rustling through the leaves. Days went by, but it did not awake. I was awake. It wasn't there anymore. I looked around cautiously, until I saw it again, towering over me. I stumbled back. Furiously, my heart leapt out of my chest. I tried to run but tripped over. It caught me, clenched me in its grip. It couldn't be human. Screaming wouldn't help. I was done for. As he lifted me towards his jaw, I woke up. Stumbling out of bed, I called for my brother Jack. As I glared, it was there...

LOUIS PRICE (13)
Hope Valley College, Hope Valley

DEAD NEIGHBOURHOOD

I found myself running from them, the cuts on me stung from their scratches and my carelessness. It hurt, but I had to go on with her, my partner that is. Her name is Sarah, she found me escaping while they chased me through the streets. We had hardly any ammo for our Ml1911s. we needed shelter.
The next day, we finally got away from the evil, ugly, disgusting beast, now we could rest.
Soon after, Sarah and me went out cautiously because of the fiends around us. I lost her... gone. She wasn't near but they were so close...

CONNOR CALLAGHAN-GRATTON (13)
Hope Valley College, Hope Valley

APOCALYPSE

'You've got to make it, you have to!' I screamed. It was too late, he'd gone.
A few hours ago, Peter and I were running for our lives. Peter had lost his. A hoard of zombies were after us. One grabbed Peter's leg violently. The others screaming in delight.
'Get to Washington. Go!'
I couldn't hold back the tears. I saw the zombies ripping him to shreds, but for me, the apocalypse had only just begun...

JADE PATRICIA DUCE (12)
Hope Valley College, Hope Valley

THE CUNNING PLAN

It all happened a long time ago. We lived in a cottage in the wood, like most wolves did.
One day, I opened the door to my house to find a girl in red next to my family's dead bodies. Like a flash, she ran out of the door.
A few years later, I saw that girl again but, just like last time, she got away. Until the day I thought of a cunning plan to get revenge for my family's deaths.

BEN ARNOLD (13)
Hope Valley College, Hope Valley

PRESSURE

I woke up. The room was a metallic, rust-orange, spreading in a melancholy atmosphere throughout the air. I remembered nothing and desperately attempted to recall my name.
Elsa. Attempting to rise, I fell back and glimpsed the viciously spiked chains wrapped around my wrists, like two pythons, crushing and suffocating its prey. Suddenly, a screen flickered on and Shrek appeared holding a leather whip. He whispered, 'What are you doing in my swamp?' The screen blanked out, my legs tingled. Then the pain crawled through my arms and stomach, veins and organs. Suddenly my body imploded under the intense pressure...

FELIX FERNANDEZ-ARIAS
Hope Valley College, Hope Valley

COLD MANSION

An ice-cold shiver brushed past my hair, giving me a disturbing chill. The moon shone fluorescent through the dark sky. Slowly I pushed open the wooden door which clung onto its hinges. As the door of the deserted house opened, before my eyes was an old-fashioned hallway. There again was the cold shiver. As I curiously ventured through the house, something warm dripped from the ceiling onto my head. From the corner of my eye, blood dripped down my cheek. Without doubt, I stormed up the stairs. As the eerie clock chimed, the knife struck my chest...

OLI JAMES (12)
Hope Valley College, Hope Valley

Nightmare

The night was quiet. As I was falling asleep I noticed a roaring sound getting louder by the second. Then the sky erupted with gunfire. A loud *clink* came from the street below. Followed by a loud hissing sound. Gas snaked into my room. There was nowhere to hide. Instinctively, I put on my gas mask, but it was too late. I gasped for air. I woke up...

DOMINIC GLANVILLE (13)
Hope Valley College, Hope Valley

As Good As Gold

A fair lady loitered, not detecting the time - late. Down steps she ran, to her shrub. 'Potions work. Lucifer may rise upon me!' Then she heard rustling...
'You spin gold from straw?' it whispered.
She was bemused. But they soon had a deal.
'Your power for this envelope, holding your wishes.'
It was agreed... She followed him but something caught her; he didn't notice. It got dark and cold, she fell asleep but woke against a wall.
'What's your name?' a figure murmured. 'I want your golden hair Rapunzel.'
There was a misunderstanding, it wasn't hair, it was straw!

MOLLIE MELLORS (14)
Kirk Hallam Community Academy, Ilkeston

THE LITTLE GIRL WITH THE THREE BEARS

A girl with long, beautiful blonde locks, was wandering through the dark and scary wood. At the end of the wood she came to a little hut. She opened the door, walked in and there, eating their breakfast, were two big, grumpy bears. The little girl quickly turned around and tried to escape, but the door slammed shut and there, behind the door, was a little bear. She was so scared when all three bears stood and walked to her, but was surprised. They said, 'Why don't you come and sit down?'

SIAN TURNER (12)
Kirk Hallam Community Academy, Ilkeston

JILL AND THE MILLIONS

Jack and Jill went up the hill to fetch a pail of water, but... then Jill pushed Jack down the well to get the inheritance of their rich parents. As Jack fell down the well, he saw his parents at the bottom and Jack shouted at Jill. Jill put the lid on the well and buried it. She got millions from the inheritance and blew it all on teddy bears and a roller coaster so she could ride the roller coaster and land in a pit of teddies she's gathered together... It ended badly.

SAMUEL BIRKIN (12)
Kirk Hallam Community Academy, Ilkeston

THE THREE LITTLE LAMBS FLUFF

Once there lived three little lambs fluff. The grass was dry so they decided to go across the bridge to eat the lush grass, but they saw a troll. 'Go away, or you're dinner!' the troll bellowed. So the lambs scrammed. This continued every day, until the biggest lamb was starving. He charged across the bridge to the other side, followed by the other two lambs; knocking the troll into the river. The three little lambs fluff were happily sleeping in the lush field that night, when a tractor came and ran them over. That was the end of them!

ELLIE JARVIS (11)
Kirk Hallam Community Academy, Ilkeston

REBELLIOUS RAPUNZEL

Rapunzel was up to no good. She had not been 18 for three days and was out of control. The witch was having no more. 'Heavens above, free me from this curse,' the witch wailed in her magic mirror as she sat with her arms shielding her head. Suddenly, she noticed an unfamiliar sound, she heard silence. The witch rushed out her room and saw the window wide open. As she approached the window, she saw Rapunzel climbing down by her hair and onto the back of a prince's horse. Rapunzel laughed as she galloped away and the witch screamed.

LILY POTTER (14)
Kirk Hallam Community Academy, Ilkeston

WITCH HUNTRESS

I smelt the musty scent of witchcraft. Whipping out my axe, the blades glistening even in the dull sunlight. The screech of the witch empowered me. Spell. Dodge. But then some dirty dust blinded me; a chain hit me to the floor, hard. Faintly a chime of a music box rang in my ears. I was losing consciousness. Though it didn't stop me. I kicked toward the looming figure, next, jumping up, swinging aimlessly with my axe, slicing straight through the skin and bone of her neck. Decapitating. Blood spattering. The deed was done. Fear me, Gretel, the witch huntress.

GEORGIA MONSHEIMER (14)
Kirk Hallam Community Academy, Ilkeston

REFLECTION OF EVENTS

I'm you. I'm your insecurities. All of your worst flaws. Your fears, worries and haunting nightmares. I'm the light, I comfort you when your soul is down. I smile when you smile. I convince you that this life we live is worth continuing. I'm the all-seeing eye; aware of all you see and do, think and feel, hope and dream. I'm nothing but a fool, a trickster. All that you live and breathe is a web of lies I've created. I'm the spider, you're the fly. These are your wishes, I tell the lies. Mirror, mirror on the wall...

NATASHA BURTON (13)
Kirk Hallam Community Academy, Ilkeston

THE CHANGING

The lightning crashed! Screaming! Crying! That was the only things I heard. I tried to run away, but I just couldn't. My parents fled and I was left alone. My legs, shivering, I just didn't know what to do. *Boom!* The sky roared with its gigantic mouth and its electrifying spit struck me! I dropped, hopeless of waking again. I could hear my heartbeat gradually getting slower and slower. The lightning shocked me again. I was out! Incredibly, the spit electrocuted my heart; I woke up. But not as me, fire came out of my head. What was I?

ISAAC ZIA
Littleover Community School, Derby

SILENCE

It was there, on its own, not a single creature was seen around it. The wooden door creaked open, which allowed me in. I cautiously glanced at the walls, which were mouldy with water dripping down them. At the corner of my eye, I saw the rocking chair moving from side to side. *Bang!* I heard something fall to the ground, I immediately caught sight of it. Slowly and steadily, I took small steps towards something strange that was happening. I felt dizzy. *Boom!* There I was, flat on the ground, closing my eyes as slow as a snail. Absolute silence...

ROSHNA SAMEE (12)
Littleover Community School, Derby

THE TEDDLY TALE

A teddy and a girl were best friends. They did everything together, played games, ate dinner and went to school. After a long day, they went to sleep in their cosy bed.

One night, the little girl heard strange noises.

The next morning, she woke up and saw something move. Its features resembled her teddy. She told her mum, but her mum didn't listen.

The following night she woke up... and died. Blood rushed out of her chest. A pointed dagger was stuck there. The teddy was standing over her, humming sinisterly. Then it disappeared as if it was magic!

SAARAH LAYLAA AHMED (12)
Littleover Community School, Derby

BLOODY MARY

I walked into the room. The lights off. The door closed. I shouldn't have done this, but I did. I looked into the mirror and said it - 'Bloody Mary, Bloody Mary, Bloody Mary.' I waited, then something gripped me and that was when she took me. Screaming for my life, she took me into her world... the dark side. I heard cries as she dragged me into the dark world. I could do nothing, say nothing, think nothing. Until I sat up from my dream. I was alive. It was Friday morning. Good.

JAYA SOOR (12)
Littleover Community School, Derby

She And He

He was the only person she could trust, although he was hairy and smelly, he was perfect in her eyes. He was fit and healthy, his body shone. She approached him cautiously, he saw her. He followed her down the stony road. She could hear his footsteps moving closer to her. She loved him so much. She reached out and stroked his face. He picked her up, she swung her arms round his neck. She put all her trust in him. He put all his trust in her. How can horses and humans love each other so much?

Lydia Haine (11)
Littleover Community School, Derby

The Killer Reflection

She was there. Her eerie presence haunting the atmosphere, her deathly gaze possessing all that came near. Her black cloak, not a crease in sight. Then there was the mirror, the mirror that always reflected her repulsive figure. The mirror that she never, ever let go of from her veined, wrinkled, witch-like hands.
For the 50th time that day, she examined herself. However, this time it was different. This time the mirror reflected her gaze back at her. With that she toppled to the ground. Her wispy, blonde hair spreading across the immaculate floor. Now she herself was possessed!

Tianna Rai (12)
Littleover Community School, Derby

THE MYSTERY OF THE GOLDEN GIRL

'Oh no, this porridge is too hot and this porridge is too cold and there's no point trying the middle one. I'll just eat my apple.'
As the bears were about to enter they heard a crash. They looked through a hole. Through the hole they saw a strand of golden hair which was as bright as the sun. They entered cautiously, unaware of who was there. They entered the living room and saw a girl having a tea party. They joined her. However, she had other plans, She dashed to the door, but never managed to escape...

MANVIR DHILLON (11)
Littleover Community School, Derby

THE MURDER OF THE PHONE GUY

Night 1 - Freddy looked around. Everything was fine. Bonnie and Chica weren't fussed. They knew he was analysing his prey.
Night 2 - Freddy knew what they were thinking. 'Done yet?' echoing in his mind.
Night 3 - Freddy knew it had to be done. Bonnie and Chica were holding in their anger. 'Soon,' he said.
Night 4 - Freddy was waiting for the power to run out. The lights were flickering on and off. Then - complete darkness. Freddy walked into the office and pounced on the unsuspecting security guard. It was over, the deed was done.

HELEN ELISE HOANG (11)
Littleover Community School, Derby

23

Furry Monster

Bang, smash, bang! Shattered glass everywhere. *Creak!* Footsteps were heard. The intruder caught a scent. It was coming from the kitchen. The scent was getting stronger and stronger, it was delicious porridge. Furry Monster couldn't resist it. Tasting them one by one, his slimy tongue got all bitter. Rushing to the refrigerator for a drink, his strength had broken the chair as well as the refrigerator door. Waking up, Blondie came rushing downstairs. Furry Monster didn't know what to do! Rushing to the exit... Blondie threatened to call the police. With a whimper Furry Monster turned and fled in horror!

JASKARAN SINGH CHHOKER (11)
Littleover Community School, Derby

Beauty And The Feast

I am at dinner; the food is nice. Beast isn't eating as much as he usually does. Maybe there's something wrong. I give him a smile and he violently flips the table over. He has an evil look in his eye and a smile on his face. My body quivers with fear. Lumiere and Chip attack me with violent punches whilst Beast ties me to a chair. He walks slowly over, knocks me half unconscious. He takes a step closer, his shining eyes getting closer and closer. He looks at me with hungry eyes and takes a threatening bite...

TONI MAYNARD (14)
Lodge Park Academy, Corby

UNTITLED

A wardrobe they said. I open the door and the walls throb red. I walk in, expecting lovely, grassy fields. Except I am wrong. I step out into the lion's den. Literally. I open my eyes only to see a massive lion giving me front row seats to his glaring white teeth. I fear for my life. I jump to my feet. My legs shake and almost collapse beneath me. He eyes me up with his giant, beady eyes. I turn to run and he begins his chase. Is it too late?

STUART SHARKEY (14)
Lodge Park Academy, Corby

THE COMMONER

Walking through the market. There, a beautiful commoner. A street rat, just like me. Roaming the streets dressed in a graceful, blue, flowing gown. I saw a glistening come from her pocket. I approached to converse with the gorgeous girl. She turned around, reached into her rear pocket and pulled out a dagger as sharp as the spindle on a spinning wheel. She plunged the dagger into my chest. She whispered, 'If only there was someone out there who loved you.'

HOLLY MCCONNELL (14)
Lodge Park Academy, Corby

25

THE FOX AND THE GINGERBREAD MAN

Tip tap, tip tap, the freshly baked gingerbread man approaches. My nose twitches, my mouth salivates, my eager eyes widen. Will my patience pay off? *Tip tap, tip tap,* the sound of him approaching makes my hair stand on end. But, the noise stops... I lay here, silent, blending in with the grass. What was that? Oh, just the wind, I shiver and feel goosebumps on my skin. My body suddenly fills with fear, I turn and, to my surprise, my prey looks me in the eye. His eyes red, mouth open... he swallows me whole. *Gulp!*

ANDREA FELICIANO (14)
Lodge Park Academy, Corby

UNTITLED

Whoosh! The wind whistled through the air. Or was it the wind? A ferocious howl met my ears, it was a recognisable howl. It was the wolf. *Crash!* The door fell down and the wolf rushed in as fast as lightning. I pierced my dagger-like teeth into his sickening skin. Crimson-red blood exploded everywhere. The bite proved to be fatal and the wolf dropped to the ground. Stone cold. No breathing. I let out a heroic roar in celebration of the end of the wolf. It was the end of a nightmare for me, but was it over?

DANIEL GOODSIR (14)
Lodge Park Academy, Corby

THE CHOCOLATE WARDROBE

Bob, Jim and Jamima hear a noise from the wardrobe and go to investigate. When they open the doors they all pile in. The next minute they are sliding down a black hole for what seems like forever. Eventually there is a light at the end of the tunnel. They go through a white twister and they pop up in Willy Wonka's chocolate factory. Mr Wonka gives them a tour and he seems normal, but all of a sudden he turns around and his eyes are devil-red. He pins them to the conveyor belt and turns them into chocolate.

JASMIN BURGIN (14)
Lodge Park Academy, Corby

BELLE THE BEAST

There he was, amazing, wonderful, beautiful! All I want is for someone to look beyond my hairy, horrendous appearance - a beast - and into my soul. Why me? Who else looks like this? I'll go, I'll see him, just talk. He's coming over, but looks straight to the Princess Rapunzel; with her flowing hair, fair skin and rosy lips, he didn't notice me. Off they go into the sunset for their happily ever after. Not me. I will get my prince. *Bang!* The dagger plunges into Rapunzel's heart, dead. Now for my happily ever after.

EMILY ILKO (13)
Lodge Park Academy, Corby

UNTITLED

My Jasmine. I can't wait. The birds will sing, beautiful peace. Anyone would die to have her. Her long, ebony hair sweeps down her back, her lovely caramel skin is irresistible. Who? Who? I hear the footsteps, *tap, tap tap*. The door opens. A ring! How preposterous is this? A diamond, my eyes must be deceiving me. She has wed without my approval! Her secretive ways haunt me. She likes to see me like this. But I'm determined to find her fiance. Where's Raza. 'Come Raza.' Where could he be?

FRANCES MCCUSKER (14)
Lodge Park Academy, Corby

WITCH KILLERS

We ran away my sister and I, deep into the woods. Never to be seen again. After days waiting, we came across a house. 'Is that Candy?' Candy! I walked over and took a bite. A witch; ugly, warty witch with a cackling laugh.
'Ha, ha, ha, ha,' she repeats over and over again.
A crossbow? I grabbed it. I killed the witch with the bolt, piercing her cold, black heart. *Splat!*
As she fell to the ground blood spilled and spewed everywhere. My sister and I ate her house. Then left, never to be seen again.

CHLOE MEAKINS (14)
Lodge Park Academy, Corby

UNTITLED

I lay here, collecting dust every second. Never to be used again. Suddenly I hear footsteps. Quiet at first, slowly getting louder and louder. Then I see a face, a hand reaching out towards me, unexpectedly grabbing me. Out of nowhere I am moving again, Flying around the room - I feel I had never stopped. A voice calls out, making me fall to the ground. I look and see confusion written on his face. I can see the questions filling up his head as I drag myself along the floor making my way towards him.

ELOISE CORNER (13)
Lodge Park Academy, Corby

UNTITLED

Filled with hatred, envy, jealousy, dressed all in black, voice filled with anger. Her brittle hands shake as she dunks it into her precious, poisonous potion. *Splash, drip, drip, drip.* The fruit crackles as it transforms from a rich, succulent, delicious, mouth-watering fruit to a rotten, heart-stopping, envious, vile, black weapon. She leaves her castle. Walks through the forest. The birds migrate as the evilness hits them like a spear. Every step, every minute is crucial. She knocks, a girl with a pale face opens the door. She takes a bite...

CHELSEA DOE-BRUCE (14)
Lodge Park Academy, Corby

THE BIG BAD WOLF

Suddenly, a wolf ran through the deep, scary wood. Running as fast as lightning could strike, howling so loud, waking all the animals that lived in the wood. Following the wolf there was a huge animal. 'Roar, roar, roar!'
The wolf turned, staring at all angles, making sure no people or animals were following him. He started running again and he was nearly at the old, creepy house. An old lady walked past, the wolf hid behind a tree. Then he jumped behind her, she fell over screaming for help - Nobody heard her...

RACHAEL MACINNES (14)
Lodge Park Academy, Corby

EPILOGUE

Running through the long grasses and swerving zephyrs and clouds, they came, a chattering and squawking of the feast that awaited them. Streaming from the crevices and rainwater ponds of the mountains flowed their whispered tones, inaudible alone, but as one, a mighty cacophony. The times of war and hatred were a pleasure to them, they, the only victors as the battlefields which once ran red turned brown and rancid, the juices of death fuelling their innumerable lives within the bowels of creation and the soaring heights of Heaven in which they shall always dwell.

MIRIAM ALDIS (14)
Moulton School & Science College, Northampton

ONE LITTLE WOLF

The wolf hunted night after night but hadn't found anything. Suddenly, there was a deep rumble of thunder and a crackle of lightning. The wolf whimpered and stepped back.

Then, out of the darkness three little pigs stood in the mist. 'This time, you run!' bellowed the smallest.The other two whacked their oversized clubs together, hoping to scare the wolf even more.

They walked on through the wood and found the wolf's neatly made den. With one blow each, the wolf's den was in pieces on the floor. 'We aren't ones to be messed with!' they said in unison.

JESSICA LOUISE NEIL (11)
Moulton School & Science College, Northampton

SISTER RIVALRY

There was a horrible girl called Cindabella and she was lucky to be invited to the party. As Cindabella went, she caught the rich prince's eye. Cindabella had to leave quickly at 12, because she was late. She lost her glass shoe in a hurry, it fell of her slender foot. The handsome prince turned up at the girls' two-bedroomed house. Cindabella didn't answer the knock at the door, but the ugly stepsister did and automatically put the shoe on her vile foot. It fit; so the prince and the sister lived unhappily ever after.

REBECCA SIDWELL (14)
New College, Leicester

31

DESTRUCTION

There she stood, shouting across the room with the anxious glare in her eyes. The icy mansion melted as the two girls were at each others' throats. It was cracking and being destroyed. There was no hope for these stunning girls. But before the beautiful, icy, shiny, mansion disintegrated, they were still arguing, glaring at each other. The sister, Elsa, took it too far and shot her lovely sister with her magical, icy powers and she fell to the floor. As soon as this happened, the mansion collapsed and Elsa fell to her death.

CAMERON SAXTON (13)
New College, Leicester

FEET TRAUMA

A mermaid lived in the sea but wanted to live on land with smartphones. She swam to the shore every day, watching secretly. Teenagers were taking selfies or texting. The evil witch of the sea saw this through her magic bubble and hatched a plan.
The next day, the witch made a deal with Ariel, if she swapped her voice for feet and had a million Twitter followers, she would get her voice back and keep the feet. Ariel told her she couldn't sing, she was lypsynching songs from Fishtube. She never did get feet and died sad and alone.

AMY BIRD
New College, Leicester

TINDERELLA

Tinderella lived in the cottage on Greengate Lane. She was on a dating website, but never got ticked.
One day, she went online and she twitched, it turned out she had a hot prince who only lived one mile away. Prince Wilip was his name. He asked for a date at the Flaming Flamingo Bar, which was also a restaurant.
They met on Tuesday with a delightful twist. Love with their first kiss? But she was a player, she pretended she liked him. Really she hated him, she ended up slapping him and walked!

KACIE-LILY YEOMAN (12)
New College, Leicester

UNTITLED

An evil stepmother orders her husband to abandon his children in the woods. Lost and starving they stumble up to a gingerbread house. However, they are both captured by the witch. They are both persuaded she's just a sweet woman but Peri and Jack are both enslaved to do everything to help the witch out.
After some moments, Peri hears dripping noises, she assumes it's just a burst pipe. Moments go by, she then discovers the room with blood everywhere and on the floor lay the bodies of a large amount of dead children. What is to become of them?

KEIGHLYANN ANN BURT (13)
New College, Leicester

OLAF'S LAST WORDS

Anna ran across the cold, slippy ice as fast as her legs could take her. She reached Elsa's ice palace and demanded she change the weather back to summer. So Elsa did.

Everyone loved Anna and were very grateful for what she done. But she soon suffered consequences. Olaf, the snowman, her best friend couldn't survive in hot weather. Anna ran to him and panicked. She said, 'Olaf, you're melting!'

He replied weakly, 'Some people are worth melting for...'

Anna cried and screamed as she collapsed on the ground, she'd saved the town but lost her friend.

KIA BOYLES (13)
New College, Leicester

THE TRUTH BEHIND THE LITTLE MERMAID

Deep under the blue sea lived a mermaid with red hair, whose dream was to live in a whole new world. The only way to do this was to trade her voice for some legs. However, true love's kiss would break the spell. She traded her voice for some legs and left to find her prince. When she met her dreamy prince they planned to get married and have children and live happily ever after. However, on their wedding day, they had their first kiss and the girl didn't get her voice back, so she was speechless forever. Stupid prince!

TARA BLOWER (14)
New College, Leicester

THREE WORRIED PIGS

Now the straw and the wood houses had failed, the wolf's only target was the solid brick house. He was too smart to try a sturdy huff. The wolf decided that he would climb down the chimney and pummel them from inside. At the top he darted down with claws ready as they pierced into the floor. He grabbed the first pig, leaving ruby blood everywhere. Darting around the room to catch the second, the wolf came to a surprise, *snap!* The wolf's head rolled across the room as the frightened pigs dropped an axe on his neck!

JOSH ANDERSON (14)
New College, Leicester

DON'T BE LATE

Cinderella got to the ball. Her fairy godmother granted her wish. She had to be home by twelve.
At the ball she was the best dressed and all eyes were on her. But not all good ones. She found the love of her life, but it was coming up to twelve, she stayed out later, but would be sorry for it.
The ball was over and her Prince Charming promised to watch over her. Little did she know, she was better off alone... The dress stained rusty red, with only her Prince Charming and her glass slipper to blame!

ABBIE MARSHALL (14)
New College, Leicester

35

SMALL EVIL

One day Snow White, the young, homeless woman, needed some help. She went to see the dwarfs who lived in a forest which was dark and mystical, very scary. The trees sounded like they were laughing at you when you walked by. Without hesitation, she knocked on a little door. She strolled in and never came running out. People were searching for her. She was never found. Who would have thought some innocent dwarfs killed her? They look harmless, but they are evil!

REECE HOOKWAY (13)
New College, Leicester

LET IT GO

One cold, frozen night, Elsa and Anna were strolling through the thick snow until they both stopped and looked at each other. They said, 'Do you wanna build a snowman?'
They both giggled. Suddenly a stormy cloud came across Emmerdale and made everything dull. Just then, a man on a horse came towards them. It was Prince Hans ready to slaughter Princess Anna. But Elsa was not going to leave them alone. Anna and Hans were arguing. Elsa was thinking, then she used her magic power to freeze Hans. But was it Hans? No! It was Anna. She was dead.

MAISIE-MAE DANCE (13)
New College, Leicester

THE GIRL WHO KILLED HER GRANDMA

The girl in the rosy red dress, her mum told her to take some cake to her grandma. Her grandma was a vile old lady.
On the way to her grandma's she bumped into a fox. But she ignored it and marched faster. As she started marching faster, she was thinking about killing her grandma and blaming it on the fox. She came up with an outstanding plan. She poisoned the cake and gave it to her grandma and because Grandma ate the cake she died. But the fox could smell it and it passed out next to Grandma!

LILLI-MAE OWEN (14)
New College, Leicester

THE BEAUTY HAS GONE

One day, Belle and the beast were in the garden and Belle saw the flowers were missing. So they went into the forest to find the flowers. The Beast saw an amazing, beautiful flower and touched it, but he didn't know it was dangerous. The Beast felt hungry for beauty. Belle shouted, 'I found the flowers.'
They went home. Belle saw something was wrong with Beast and she was scared for him and herself. Belle told Beast to go away, but he didn't listen to her. He walked towards her, she screamed - then silence.

SARAH JANE OSBORNE (14)
New College, Leicester

THE LONELY GIRL

A girl with long, flowing, silky hair, went out of the dark and isolated tower with a well-known thief. When they got out the thief left her alone in the cruel world. Her horrible, selfish mother took her back to the isolated tower and made her do all the housework.
One day, the girl couldn't take it anymore and pushed her mum, not realising that she was near the window. She killed her. Now she was finally free from her evil mother, but she was lost in the world.

CHARLOTTE WHITBY (13)
New College, Leicester

THE INNOCENT DEMON

I can smell them miles away. The thought of pepper-soup with innocent souls dazzles me with joy. They're nearly here and I've got to get ready. I turn my evil lair into a normal home. I open the door with Hansel looking beaten up and Gretel looking like the devil in disguise with an evil undercurrent. I wonder if Hansel feels it too? Gretel's eyes start glowing red, it takes me minutes to realise she is releasing her demon without warning. I'm blasted high into the air, my last thought is there is a demon in everyone!

MANUELA NKRUMAH (13)
New College, Leicester

REVENGE OF THE INNOCENCE

Everyone has a demon inside them!
Little Red Riding Hood ran with no fear whatsoever. Her prey was only trees away now! She had been waiting for this time to come for years... now it had finally arrived. Screams echoed up and down the creepy, dark forest. As she spun with her red cloak all that was left was a dead woman whom she called her grandma. There was no fear, there was no smell - but there was a lot to see - Would she ever get caught?

SAKSHI PALA (14)
New College, Leicester

THE GIRL WHO POISONED HERSELF

Once upon a time there was a wolf who could smell fresh blood. A red-hooded girl promenaded down a narrow road as she was collecting precious mushrooms for her elderly, grey-haired grandmother. As she foot-slogged along the restricted path, she got ravenous. She took a voluminous bite out of a mushroom. She started to feel light-headed so she sat down and fell asleep. A venerable lady walking past tried waking the girl but she wouldn't wake up. The wolf let her be.

JANE STATHAM (14)
New College, Leicester

THE AWOKEN GOAT

Once upon a time, there was a queen who lived in a castle. She didn't have a king.

One day, a witch, disguised as a small girl, gave the queen a basket full of mangoes. She ate the whole basketful, even the basket. She slept after eating.

Next day, she was found asleep. After 1,000 years she woke and saw herself in the mirror. She looked like a goat. She was afraid of herself. She became that angry, she destroyed Pluto, the planet and then she calmly played the goat simulator in real life.

Then, she lived happily.

RAUNAK SACHIN SOMAN (12)
New College, Leicester

BEAUTY AND THE BEAST

'A beast, I'm horrible, I need her!'

Beauty being my twin sister, separated at birth, I'm out hunting, looking for fresh meat.

'What's that smell? It's a girl riding on a horse.'

I'm turning, she sees me and gestures with her hand. 'Come with me.' We soon come to her house. I see him, he realises who I am. Then Beauty questions him. Shock is tempting, I turn into the beast. She grabs weapons, slashing me, I fall, dead.

She runs to my castle and kills herself in regret. You can still hear her when she is close enough.

SIAN KELB (12)
New College, Leicester

PETER PAN RETURNS WORSE THAN EVER

Once upon a time, Wendy was doing her school work when Peter Pan flew in the room. Wendy knew him from previous adventures and knew he meant no harm, or did he?
Peter Pan scooped Wendy up in his arms and flew to Neverland, a place Wendy knew well. She almost died there along with Tiger Lily. Wendy was dreading this. She didn't know what to do or say. She just screamed, hoping to go back home. Peter would not let her go home and kept her captive. Soon enough she was dead. Peter Pan had killed Wendy Darling!

TIA-ROSE JOHNSON (12)
New College, Leicester

WHO NEEDS A MAN?

Cinderella was sick and tired of doing her stepfamily's chores. Her loneliness had grown, slaughtering the mice was boring. She had to kill them!
Later that night Cinderella slaughtered her stepfamily, *Who needs a man?* she thought. Unfortunately there's always a consequence for a bad deed.
In the mad house Cinderella screamed, 'I'm not a slave!'
Every time a doctor asked her questions, she laughed in their faces. Finally she escaped! Wondering what would entertain her, she saw a poster, displaying the name 'One Direction'. Cinderella swore that their blood would be on her hands. Will she realise her wish?

GRACIE-MAE ALANA YATES (12)
New College, Leicester

Cinderella's Big Disaster

Cinderella had an evil stepmother and two ugly stepsisters. The ugly stepsisters were going to the ball and Cinderella really wanted to go. Her fairy godmother whispered, 'You shall go to the ball.' Then she turned a pumpkin into a big coach, turned the mice into the horses and finally Cinderella's rags into a big, blue dress.

The night of the ball, Cinderella turned up and had a blast and remembered she had to leave before 12. The clock struck 12 and she dashed out. The horses turned into the face of her perfect, handsome prince.

They happily got married!

ELLIE WILSON (12)
New College, Leicester

A Kiss To Save A Life

Once upon a time there was a prince. He had a crush on an old witch who sold apples for a living.

One day, the prince finally gathered the confidence to ask the witch on a date and she said yes!

When he arrived at the restaurant, she handed him an apple filled with green goop! He went home later that night, feeling like death. He went straight to bed -

20 years later... *Boom!* The door swung off its hinges. A princess, dressed in a ninja suit, burst into the room and kissed the prince to save his life!

MADISON MADELIN (12)
New College, Leicester

THE TRAGIC DEATH OF ALICE

Once, there was a girl called Alice who fell down a rabbit hole. After a while of being there, she started to get hungry and wanted to eat. Surprisingly, on a biscuit it said, *Eat Me*. So obviously she ate it. As she swallowed she started to shrink. Suddenly, a huge bird came down and grabbed her and took her up into the blue sky. Alice was screaming her head off. She wanted to go down and struggled to get free. The bird immediately knew what she was thinking and released her, so she dropped to her tragic death.

CAITLIN LOCKE (12)
New College, Leicester

CINDER

Once upon a time there lived a man called Cinder. He was a cleaner at McDonald's. He'd had enough and wanted to go and be a night club owner.
On Saturday night he went to the Glass Slipper in town. He danced all night to Eminem and got totally drunk. Little did he know he'd lost his right Nike Air.
He got home, took his shoe off and went to bed.
On Sunday, he was woken by a knock on the door. It was the night club owner with the Nike. It fitted and they lived in New Parks together.

SUMMER FLECK (12)
New College, Leicester

CINDER'S MURDER

Once upon a time, in a gloomy forest, Cinderella sat. But back at the house were two beautiful stepsisters. They called Cinderella and she sprinted to the house. They told her to do the washing. But then a letter came for the ball. The two stepsisters left for the ball as Cinderella's fairy godmother came. She wished for a grenade gun and she ran to the ball. She launched grenades in the castle and watched her two stepsisters get blown and torn to pieces. Cinderella's eyes turned red and she never lived happily ever after!

LISA WHITE (13)
New College, Leicester

GINGERBREAD MAN RULES THE WORLD

Once upon a time there lived a gingerbread called Ginger and he was a secretly trained assassin who killed predators.
One day, a cow tried to eat poor Ginger, but the cow was in for a big, shocking surprise. The cow fell to the floor because he was machine-gunned. Next, the fox tried to kill the hidden assassin Ginger, but again the fox got a deadly surprise of death. So no one ever tried to kill Little Ginger again. But Ginger was prepared to kill anyone in his path, so everyone but Little Ginger didn't live happily ever after.

BROGAN COUSINS (12)
New College, Leicester

THE STORY OF CINDY

Once upon a time there was a girl called Cindy. She lived with her stepmum and her evil sisters.

One day she was invited to a party. She was excited. Sadly her stepmum said her sisters needed to go with her. She got ready. After the party she tried to find her phone. Her sister kept putting her down. Finally she stood up for herself and killed her sisters and stepmum. She lived in her stepmum's house.

A mysterious man kept on stalking her.

One day he gave her her phone back. They married each other and lived in joy.

ROKSANA JASKROWSKA (11)
New College, Leicester

GOLDILOCKS AND THE THREE CARE BEARS

Once upon a time there was a girl called Goldilocks. She had nowhere to sleep and no food, only the berries that grew on the trees.

One day, she saw that there was an open door. Nobody was there, except her. It was the perfect house. No taxes to pay, beds, food in the fridge. Everything. But who's this? A pink one, a blue one and a green one. Care Bears!

Goldilocks hadn't eaten any breakfast that morning. The softness was getting to her. She couldn't help herself. No more Care Bears were to live in this house again. Eaten!

KATIE DIXON (11)
New College, Leicester

PETER'S PLAN

Anna sat there wondering what to do. Just then, a boy called Peter Pan glided through the window. He asked Anna if she wanted to fly with him. He put too little powder on Anna, she didn't notice! As she lunged herself from the window, she fell to the ground.

In the undergrowth of Earth, Anna became a terrifying demon. She realised that Peter Pan had killed her, so she killed him. She felt good, evil, like that demon what she was born to be. Then, with that, she lunged from the ground, glided up and killed the world!

JOANNE KAVENAGH (11)
New College, Leicester

CINDERELLA WITH A TWIST

Cind's stepbrothers and father didn't want him at the night club, The Glass Slipper, so his family locked him in a closet. However, his pet mice helped him out. Cind really wanted to go to the Glass Slipper. Suddenly, *poof!* A guy in a pink ball gown had appeared. 'I am your fairy godfather,' he exclaimed. 'I heard you wanted to go to the night club.'

So he magicked up a Bugatti made from a pumpkin. He also gave Cind some new clothes and some sneakers. 'Be back by 12 or else something bad will happen!'

HARISA ALI (12)
New College, Leicester

ALONE

Alone, he was alone. Desperately in need of warmth, he was now roaming through what was fantasised to be civilisation. As he stared at the pitch-black sky, he felt the presence of another. As if he was being... watched. His breathing increased dramatically, he was petrified, searching for whatever it was in an endless loop of insanity. There was a snarl from inside the lifeless trees. He heard subtle but powerful steps approaching. He tried to move but he couldn't. He was frozen. Now visible were piercing green eyes. It pounced. The last thing he saw was scarlet-red. Alone.

JAMES FORREST (13)
New College, Leicester

UNTITLED

They're coming slowly. They come in packs, hunting. Their blood-red eyes following, stalking, waiting to change their fur black as night. You cannot tell them from the midnight sky, they scrounge on the bodies of the dead. They feed on the fear of the living. They're closing in. They don't know what I am, they think I'm just a young girl dressed in red. But when they near they will see my real identity. My eyes go black, my fangs come out, I grow taller every second. My thirst for blood becomes greater. Then I strike - no more wolves!

MARSHALL BREWIN (13)
New College, Leicester

THE DISAPPEARANCE

In the forest a mysterious shadow lurks around, waiting for a victim to join it. No one dares step foot in the dark deathtrap! Until one day, a boy came looking for firewood. He saw the shadow creeping up to him. He shouted, 'Who's there?' *Swoosh!* The trees shook as the cold wind brushed across the boy's face. The black shadow circled the boy. He stood there mumbling, with nothing but crows, bats and fear around him. He was gone!
People still wonder what happened to the poor, innocent boy to this day, since he'd disappeared without a trace.

MADISON ANDERSON (13)
New College, Leicester

THE WITCH OF WATERSTONE HOUSE

'Waterstone House' it reads. I walk to the door. *Knock, knock.* No answer. I knock again, the door swings open! I gasp, looking for the culprit. No one's there. As I walk inside the door slams shut behind me. I spin round to witness no door! A chair with a doll sitting on it faces me. It's an old doll, ragged clothes, dull hair, its eyes have been removed. I walk into the next room, I see a girl looking into a globe. I remember the first time I saw that girl and that globe. Another poor soul is lost.

ERIN BENNETT (12)
New College, Leicester

SNOW'S TWIST

Bang! Crackle! Pop! Bent over a cauldron, she brewed a sleeping potion. What she didn't know was on the other side of the deep, dark forest, Snow White had a few ideas of her own.

Upon Snow's arrival at the woman's house, Snow White crept through the door. Trying not to make a sound, she tiptoed to the woman's bed. As Snow White turned to grab something, *chomp!* Snow White fell to the floor screaming. Out jumped the wolf, he looked directly at her. He said, 'She knew you were coming...' Nobody saw Snow White again!

LAURA MCKEOWN (13)
New College, Leicester

THE GRIM REAPER

The king leapt up. On his face there was the hint of alarm. Right there stood his most feared foe.

'You!' shouted the king. His voice echoed past the throne room and into the hall. Standing before him, in a black cape, was the Grim Reaper.

He spoke in a sinister voice, 'Your time has come, right after I finish eating my apple.'

They battled with platinum swords until the king finally hit him in the stomach. The Grim Reaper laughed as his wounds healed. To the king's horror, he himself was dying. One minute later the king died.

JUSTIN GEORGE (12)
New College, Leicester

THE HOUSE

At the end of the street an old house was up for sale. Weeks later, a rich lady had moved in and settled into her new home. One night something was lurking in the corner of the bedroom. It was a doll, a doll she'd had since she was seven. Its eyes were deep blue, its hair drooped over them like a curtain.
That night, Crystal heard a noise, scratching. She was in shock. All of a sudden the doll rose from the chair and took over Crystal's soul. To date, the doll continues to roam the streets of London.

OLIVIA YATES (12)
New College, Leicester

THE EVIL QUEEN

Dark. Nobody. Everything seemed to be quiet. Suddenly I heard a sound. I shivered. I walked down the wood, I couldn't see anything. I heard the sound of footsteps, I turned round. Nothing. Someone was following me. As I tried to find out who it was, I saw a light that shimmered brightly at the far end. When I walked towards the spot, the sound of the footsteps got louder. I stopped. Then looked. Nobody. I continued walking - I got closer. There! A flash of white light coming towards me, almost blinding me. There I saw... the Snow Queen.

ANN THOMAS (13)
New College, Leicester

THE MONSTER I'VE BECOME

The enchanted forest, 1918. *Splash!* Ariel swam. After making a deal with Ursula she had to swim fast. Her teeth grew pointier, her tail disappeared. Unable to breathe, Ariel's body weakened. Ariel made it to land just in time, she was no longer a mermaid, she was a vampire! Hiding constantly until she saw him. Captain Blackbeard, mightiest killer and scoundrel, known to mankind. Ariel made a deal with the sinister pirate. She had asked for a potion that would help her stop draining blood from innocent villagers. All she wanted was adventure, now she's got a gory, horrendous reputation!

MEGAN JONES (13)
New College, Leicester

THE GIRL... OR IS SHE?

There she is. The most beautiful, wonderful girl I've ever seen. I don't have the guts to talk to her. I love her luxurious blonde hair and pretty pink dress. I guess she's going for the lead, any girl like her would get it. Should I go, or should I stay? If I go, what do I say? Now's the time. I walk toward her, tap her on the shoulder, here goes. 'Er...' She turns around. 'Hi?' she says with a deep voice like a boy. I don't think she's a girl, she's a he and he's a boy!

SHANNON RICHARDS
New College, Leicester

THE MISTAKE

In a wood, not far from here, a wolf was lurking, hunting for its prey.
The sun went down and the moon came up. The forest went black,
the trees were crackling like shooting popcorn.
'Oowwoo!'
He smelt his first victim. He sprinted, the scent was getting closer. He
stopped. The scent had ended. All he could smell now was sloppy,
wet mud. The small girl turned, her face appeared green, with two
pointed ears. She smiled, mud dripped from her mouth. The wolf
looked up extremely surprised and gulped as the girl screamed. The
wolf yelped and darted away.

KIERAN HOOD (12)
New College, Leicester

UNTITLED

Simba reappears. The whole city's future in his hands. Now it was all
down to him. Scar stood there, in the mist, Simba was ready now, or
as ready as he was going to be.
Suddenly, *whoosh!* Half of the city went up in scorching, bright red
flames. It was time. Time for the duel, young children and mothers
stood and watched the future and the city was all riding on this
battle. *Bang!* The duel was over and the crown was Simba's. The
crowd cheered with relief. The duel was over, but it wasn't, it had just
begun...

ELOISE WIGNALL (13)
New College, Leicester

UNTITLED

Boom, boom, boom! She knocked on the door; it creaked open. Goldy looked around, making sure nobody was there. She slowly stumbled into the mysterious house, not knowing what was to come. She went in, then, suddenly, *bang!* The portrait fell off the wall! Goldy picked it up; she looked at the face and it looked familiar, she knew that she'd seen it before, but where?
'Ouch!' she screamed at the top of her voice. Blood dripped off her finger and onto the floor. She dropped the portrait and headed towards the door. She'd seen them!

HRITIKA PALA (13)
New College, Leicester

DON'T GO INTO THE WOODS TODAY

The girl heard a growl, she turned around and saw a sharp-toothed wolf. The girl ran, clutching her little basket. She ran to the woods, even though she was warned not to. Her cloak flew through the wind. She looked around, scared of the things wandering around. She saw a cottage in the distance, she ran there using all her energy. She knocked on the door hastily and when it opened the girl gasped. The three bears stepped out, the wolf, standing grinning, behind them. 'No porridge,' they chanted.
All that was heard throughout the wood - was screaming.

ANGEL NORTH (13)
New College, Leicester

THE GHOSTLY BUCCANEER

The wind whipped at my jacket sleeve. The unholy mixture of salt, blood and sweat sickened me. My severed stump floated on the waves, sailing true north, until the menacing visage of the great white crested the surface and swallowed my dearly departed appendage. Across the water, standing astern, laughing, the ghostly flicker of the Buccaneer gripped my neck. But with relief I heard his mast crashing into the sea. Our gamble had worked. The hell frigate drifted away, helplessly. The hunt was just getting started. I knew it would continue throughout the seven seas and into my nightmares.

GEORGE WARREN (13)
New College, Leicester

THE MAN

The rain was getting faster, the sky darker. They saw a house in the distance, an old brick building in the mist. They approached the house. *Knock, knock.* The door slowly creaked open. A woman ran out of the house. They entered, checking everywhere for supplies and entered a dark room. They caught a glimpse of a man in the corner - they all made eye contact. The man looked terrified. He made a run for it, exiting out of an open window. He knew they were not normal people.
After that day, the two people were never seen again.

CHLOE ALDERTON (13)
New College, Leicester

THE END OF EARTH

For five nights straight, green missiles were sent from Mars, destination Earth. Is this the end of human life on Earth? People were shouting, crying and screaming for help, but no help came.
On the night of the attack, people fell on their knees as alien spaceships came. They started sucking up people through tubes. People didn't run away, they ran to the spaceships. Why? The aliens didn't want Earth, they were our saviours, but what from?
As we left for our new home, Mars, the catastrophic asteroid imploded, destroying Earth!
We wait for our new future.

ASHLEY REID (14)
New College, Leicester

THE GIRL IN THE WOODS

Awakening in the middle of the night, sweat trickles down my greasy skin. There, a beautiful girl stands right in front of me. Her black, ebony hair swaying across her face. Her skin glistening like a million diamonds. Two sharp fangs appear, she starts to approach me. I try to run, but slip and fall. I start to panic. I turn in terror, she's getting closer, she stops, she points towards the trees. I'm surrounded by sixty, ferocious vampires. They're all covered in... something red; flesh and blood. The smile at me, I scream. Suddenly they all pounce on me.

EMILY LOUISE GIBSON (13)
New College, Leicester

55

Rapunzel Has Gone Wrong

She turned her hair a magical glow. She looked straight at me, but there was something different, something I had never noticed before. Her eyes turned red, like the scarlet found on her magical cloak. Her teeth showed as she smiled, he fangs sticking out. It scared me, I took a step back and nearly fell out the tower!
I ran and ran ahead, as fast as I could, but she was twice as fast as me. She flew upward with her cloak and she started disappearing. She shouted, 'Wait, I will return and I will have my revenge!'

ILZE PUTNINA (13)
New College, Leicester

Plummeting

'Argh!' Falling. The height is petrifying. What is this place? Pianos, chairs, rocks split over my head. The ground is nowhere to be seen. Eyes are watching me from the walls. I scream, but it just echoes back. I hit ledges, but keep accelerating. I cannot breathe. How did I get in here? I can't remember anything. An eerie mist creates a shiver up my spine. Objects are hitting me from all angles. What are they? I can just see something. Rocks and rubble are covering it. I reach out for the ledges, but I still plummet downward. *Bang...!*

MORGAN LEE (13)
New College, Leicester

DREAMCATCHER

The machines began to turn. A spark had appeared. A spark of imagination; the first in 300 years. Beams of light flashed across the dark, dark world. With a whirr the belt creaked into shape, then turned in a rhythm of echoes.
After all, it was out of use. But it worked and it just may be the saving grace. Another burst of golden light pierced through the ever-dark sky. Euphoria danced through the factory. But it didn't last. It didn't even leave. Floating in a void of nightmares, then it stopped. The light was swallowed in the shadows. Dreamcatchers.

EVANN JOYCE (12)
New College, Leicester

THE DUNGEON

Oh no, the clock showed 11.55, five minutes. He sprinted away, trying to avoid the dreaded 12 chimes of damnation. He ran, backtracking to the safety of his cell. 11.56, this was hopeless, but he could try. He ran down a corridor - 11.57. The seconds were dissolving in his head. 11.58. No sign of help. 11.59. His heart beat like a drum. 12.00, the end. The torches stopped working, huge shadows stalked him. He ran, eyes in the silhouettes stared at him. Furniture trembled. He stopped, he knew his way now. Overjoyed he zoomed forward and... 'March!' He had failed.

LEWIS ARMITAGE (13)
New College, Leicester

THE MYSTERY DRIVE

I gradually opened my eyes, not knowing where I was. I couldn't remember what had happened, darkness towered over me. I couldn't see a thing. I heard something, I wasn't sure what it was. But then my heart sank, when I realised I was in the boot of a car. My head was dripping with blood. Had I been stabbed? Shot? I didn't know. 1,000 questions were racing through my mind, I couldn't think straight. My heart was pounding out of my chest. Suddenly the car came to a halt, we had stopped. Why? Was today my last day on Earth?

TYLA STRONG (13)
New College, Leicester

THE MAGICAL BABY

There was a creak coming from the door. There was a gust of wind that flew through the castle. A dark shadow flew up the stairs. It was the witch! She was looking for a baby with magical, golden hair. There were black flashes everywhere, she wasn't worried about the noise she made, she used her powers to make everywhere go pitch-black. She could smell where the baby was. She went to pick the baby up and she stared into its eyes. The baby's eyes went red and made her jump out the window. Blood splattered everywhere. Oops!

LEONA MARSHALL (12)
New College, Leicester

THE CLIMB

Finally I would see the girl behind the voice. Looking up at the 5,000 foot tower, I started to climb. I was nearly there, I could see the window above. Shining through was the most gorgeous hair ever. My arms started getting weaker by the second. But I carried on climbing. Suddenly, my fingers started slipping. Something was on the stone, but what? It was red. I tried to hold on, but my arms couldn't hold me much longer. As the tower got further away, the ground got closer. I looked at my fingers - purple! What was it?

CHLOE BRIERS (13)
New College, Leicester

SNOW WHITE'S BABY

Snow White was getting married to the prince when the wicked witch stormed in. She said that she was going to come the day a baby was born.
A few weeks later, the wicked witch came with her army. Snow White was giving birth to her beautiful daughter. The witch and her army were getting closer. The dragon burned down the castle gates, just as Snow White gave birth to her baby girl. The witch made her way to the room. She killed the prince and snatched the baby from Snow White. Thn she flew away and took the baby.

ELLICE HEMPHILL (12)
New College, Leicester

59

A Switch Of The Apples

Snow White turns around, picking up every piece of wood she can see. She turns to see the Queen with an apple. She tells her to eat it. Snow White says that she can't eat alone and picks another apple, offering it to the Queen. The Queen turns to go, but comes back, thinking it's the only way that Snow White will eat the apple.
By then Snow White had switched the apples, knowing that it was poisonous. They start eating, but stop. The Queen then drops dead on the floor. The Queen isn't the only evil one here now.

CAITLIN MCCABE (13)
New College, Leicester

GRACE

On that day she was no older than the scar upon my left index finger. A beacon of innocence in a world of smog and ash. She excelled under my teachings, a prodigy of the highest magnitude. She was my favourite student, and I her favourite teacher. Her betrayal came to me like a scythe to an unsuspecting throat. I rang her bell with the intention to teach, to nurture her young mind under private tutorship. What a fool I was. She handed me a drink. I gulped it down. I fell to the floor with a thud. 'To us'.

EVAN CLARK (17)
Outwood Academy Newbold, Chesterfield

GHOSTS FROM THE PAST

One night, this really young girl about four years of age went to bed and slept with her mum for the night. Her mum woke up in the middle of the night and her daughter wasn't there. She obviously was worried, so she ran to ring someone. When she went to the hall her daughter was there with her back facing towards her; she was talking to herself. The mother went up to her and started asking who she was talking to. She said, 'An old friend.' But no one was there. Her startled mum took her back to bed.

KANE THOMPSON (13)
Outwood Academy Newbold, Chesterfield

TIGER CHASE

A bloodthirsty battle between a bounty hunter and a pack of guiltless tigers had commenced. Urged to run, intimidated tigers fled through the forest. The eager murderer stalking them for his next kill. Silhouettes running through a maze of trees, desperately trying to find an exit through deathly gun shots were killing their hopes of survival. The bounty hunter was thirsty for a prize but the experienced tigers darted through every passage in the never-ending forest. The wise hunter crouched down, hiding from the exhausted pack. He loaded his jet-black pistol, took a deep breath and fired.

GEORGIA JOLLEY (11)
Outwood Academy Newbold, Chesterfield

DEATH IS COMING

Dying slowly, the old wrinkled grandma spoke to her grandson with a gentle voice, saying, 'Death is coming.' The grandson was confused and slowly walked out of the room his grandma was in, with his face trying to hold in emotion. As he walked down the steps of the house, he heard a scream from the room. She had died. He ran extremely fast up the stairs to the room to see that a devil had been eating her face. The boy screamed and legged it out the house to find that there was a devil army waiting for him.

JACK JOLLEY (11)
Outwood Academy Newbold, Chesterfield

THE ZOMBIE SURVIVAL

Today is day 28 of the England zombie survival. Our home is destroyed. We have nowhere to live. This is a nightmare, not just this but we have to fight to survive. We have weapons to kill people that turn into monsters that we call zombies. We kill and find food, also shelter to live. Every day we find survivors to make a big group to survive this nightmare.
Soon, I am the only one left, everybody has died and turned into the monsters. I am the last one standing. My only path is death, so I die.

JACK ZHANG (12)
Outwood Academy Newbold, Chesterfield

THE SEVEN MASKED ASSASSINS

The trees crowded round her, their sharp fingers reaching towards her. The girl stood hunched over, breathing heavily, each shaky breath burning her throat. The sky darkened, the sun retreating behind the snow-capped mountains, casting shadows on the forest floor. Brightly coloured flowers folded in on themselves and disappeared into the dark mist that now swirled around the hem of her silk, black mourning dress. A flock of ravens suddenly launched themselves into the air, their shrill calls alerting her. She glanced around frantically and then saw what she had been running from. The new king's seven masked assassins.

SOPHIE DRING (14)
Ratcliffe College, Leicester

A WALK IN THE MARKET
ON A SUMMER MORNING

Through the rolling tide of the market-goers, a glimpse of a small, doll-like girl is caught. As the sun's golden beams stretched forth and caressed her cheek, Asheda straightened her favourite red hijab. Sweet tones of the melody she sung could be heard over the babble and chime of the market. Exquisite scents of spices blossomed in her nose as she strolled over the mismatched cobbles to her father's house. She poked her head through the door. A man was there, wearing a sea of greens. Asheda froze. A shot ripped through the air, unheard over the crowds.

ROBYN HENDRY (15)
Ratcliffe College, Leicester

DEATH AND DOOM, ALL IN ONE PLACE

The dark, gloomy nights of Darkmore are full of hideous creatures. One night three teens, Jack, Sam and Blane, were all camping. Surrounded by forest, each hour one of them changed to watch guard. Sam was the first to watch. Twenty minutes into the watch Sam heard a noise in the bushes so he went to check. Slowly he crept towards the bush... a wild beast lunged at him. He had nowhere to run. As the beast landed it ripped him apart bit by bit until there was nothing left! The boys awoke to no Sam but death everywhere!

JOSHUA FEDORENKO (11)
Retford Oaks Academy, Retford

BACK DOWN TO THE GIRL

The wind roared. The stars shone. Blood splattered on the white snow. The wolf howled. A sweet red liquid tingling his tongue. He caught another scent and ran. With the target now in sight, he pounced through the pitch-black darkness of the night. The white snow being the only colour visible. The target was an easy catch for him but as he approached, she turned. Yes, she turned, a human. A real human in the presence of such an almighty beast. The wolf couldn't believe it, but he also couldn't attack. Such a vulnerable girl, and he couldn't attack.

LAUREN CROSS-SWAIN (11)
Retford Oaks Academy, Retford

GHOSTLY CHILLS

Sam is a young girl who lives in a lovely neighbourhood, or at least she used to. Today she is moving. It wasn't her choice, she doesn't want to but she has to. That day she arrived at the house, it didn't seem the same as when she last saw it. It gave her chills as she walked through the huge wooden door. It almost felt ghostly. As days went by, she began to feel unsafe, until one night when she awoke to a little girl screaming. That night was the last anyone saw of her.

SOPHIE DAY (12)
Retford Oaks Academy, Retford

PARTY CLOWN

Joanne and McKenzie went to a birthday party. They went to get some food but they saw a clown in the dining room. They screamed. No one heard. They ran out of the door but got trapped inside. They screamed their hearts out but still no reply. No help. No surrender. It got to midnight and the clowns came on small bikes into the kitchen with axes, knives and lots of other weapons. Then, just as they thought something was going to happen, they heard their mum say it was time to get out of bed to go to school.

BILLIE-JO ROBERTS (11)
Retford Oaks Academy, Retford

CINDERELLA

In a luminous forest behind charcoal trees, lived a girl in a cottage. Her name was Cinderella! She lived with her ugly stepsisters and her horrific mother. Longing for her prince to arrive! One day she was in the cottage doing the house work when she heard, 'Tolot - tolot.' While taking a staggering step outside, 'Come thou maid, if you step in this beautiful carriage!' She stepped in the carriage, thinking all would be well, but the only thing she didn't know was that she was going to have a head full of lead! The End!

LYDIA BAILEY (12)
Retford Oaks Academy, Retford

THE DISAPPEARANCE

There once was a witch - Gaggleheckle. One day Sarah decided to steal from the village shop, so Gaggleheckle made up the most horrendous curse. He created a monster who ate Sarah.
The next day, Gaggleheckle was in his workshop when he saw a face - the monster's face. The monster stayed there until Gaggleheckle said a name and then the monster went and ate the person. This happened every day and the villagers were so perplexed by the disappearance of everyone.
Eventually everyone was gone, even Gaggleheckle and his family. Who knows where the monster is now.

GEORGINA MACKAY (12)
Retford Oaks Academy, Retford

DANGER IN THE WOODS

It was a dark and gloomy night and there, walking through the woods, was a young, beautiful girl looking terrified and lost. Suddenly, a zombie jumped out a tree and roared. The girl screamed and ran faster than before. She made it to a small cottage, she was panting. She knocked on the door heavily, not wanting the zombie to come back. The door opened and sat in the rocking chair was a skeleton and the zombie, she was petrified. They got up, took her to a room. While she slept they attempted to kill her. She ran away rapidly!

HOPE FOX (11)
Retford Oaks Academy, Retford

THE STALKER

There he was, the stalker. Stood silently, breathing. Eyeing up his prey like a piece of meat. He could feel his sticky breath blowing back onto his cold, clammy face in the winter breeze. It wasn't long until Christmas, but the man had no family to spend it with. Perhaps this is why he takes pleasure in injecting other families with terror and pain. Hoping to make people feel like he did. He was still hiding, staring, thinking. He felt his heart racing. Only then did he know he was ready. Any minute now, any second. Suddenly he pounced...

JADEN WALTON (11)
Retford Oaks Academy, Retford

WATCH OF THE WEREWOLF

The full moon rose in the distance, casting a glow over the eerie forest. The werewolf, a strong-built monster, was savaging the bones of a deer when it heard footsteps. Its ears flickered towards the sound. *People!* It edged towards the sound, licking its lips hungrily despite the deer. Suddenly, the footsteps stopped. It cautiously rounded a corner and found two dozen people, sitting around a campfire. It prepared to spring and claim its prizes when a twig snapped underneath. The people, terrified, fled screaming. It thought, *I may not be munching bones, but screams are good enough for me.*

LAUREN ROSE EMERY (11)
Retford Oaks Academy, Retford

RAPUNZEL'S DEADLY TALE

Sat in the window by moonlight with a candle burning, she felt a sharp tug on her long, beautiful hair. Suddenly she appeared looking more haggard than usual. Her long draped cape covered her from head to toe. She pulled out a juicy red apple and turned to Rapunzel. She pushed it into Rapunzel's hands and said, 'Eat.' She did as she was told and bit down on the apple. Suddenly, she began to choke... With a cough a piece of apple flew from Rapunzel's mouth, hitting the witch in the eye. Blinded, stumbling backwards through the windows, she died.

MACY BETH CLARK (12)
Retford Oaks Academy, Retford

THE GRIM FOOTBALL GAME

One cold winter's day, John and Stuart were kicking a football in the park when suddenly the ball swerved into the nearby, gloomy forest. Luckily Stuart spotted the ball and ran towards it. In a flash, Stuart tripped over and fell down into a massive pit filled with hissing, slithering, snapping pythons. Screaming, Stuart panicked and threw the ball out of the pit. Hearing Stuart's screams, John grabbed a spiky, lethal stick and began to scare the grim, dangerous snakes away. Relieved, Stuart climbed hurriedly out of the pit and the friends returned to their game of football.

HAYDEN GREAVES (11)
Retford Oaks Academy, Retford

SNOW WHITE

Once upon a time Snow White was a young girl. She had to live with her stepmother, the wicked queen, because her dad married the queen. She was jealous because Snow White was fairer than the queen so the queen got her huntsman to take Snow White to the woods to be killed. But the huntsman didn't kill her, he gave her a poison apple; she fell to the ground and he left her there.
A few days later she disappeared and when the huntsman went back she was nowhere to be seen. She was eaten by some wolves.

TIEGAN CALDER (11)
Retford Oaks Academy, Retford

The Wolf And The Sheep

'Let's play a game,' Tanya whispered to the boy. Chad nodded. 'You can be the wolf, and I'll be the sheep.' He nodded again. 'Close your eyes, count to ten, and find me.'

The boy did and the girl ran. After a moment, he ran into the forest after her. One of the women at the party said, 'That's nice of the boy to play with his sister.'

The other woman screamed, 'She doesn't have a brother.'

Tanya was reported missing that day but she was never found. As for the boy... he was found alive.

Alex Kovacs (12)
Retford Oaks Academy, Retford

Wolf Lane

Darkness was falling over the hills as Adam played with his dog. He glanced at his watch and made his way back to his grandparent's cottage. He wasn't far away when he heard a sound coming from the bushes. He stopped for a moment, but saw nothing, then carried on. Adam got to the end of the lane, almost home, he heard a growl. He stopped and listened. Suddenly, a wolf jumped out in front of him, blocking his path. There was no way out. Adam screamed, his dog barked, the wolf snarled, and then he pounced. Adam screamed again.

Shane Lambley (11)
Retford Oaks Academy, Retford

THE PALE RIDER

A masked pale rider started a new journey, and maybe his last one... He set off in the screamers wood. His objective was to find a piece of a puzzle. The puzzle was his friend's death. He went on riding his skeleton horse. Riding. Riding. Suddenly, he heard a high-pitched scream, and within a few seconds, he and his horse were down on the floor. His horse started to turn into black fog. He was all alone now, or was he? The wood was suspiciously silent. All of a sudden, he saw a screamer, the next second, he was black-fog.

HISHAM WAFAI (12)
Retford Oaks Academy, Retford

FIGURES IN THE NIGHT

As Mary lay in her bed, the darkness of the night started to sneak close to her and as it does Mary started to feel frightened. As she started to doze off, Mary started to hear and see her mother and father come in through the door, but, the weird thing is that they were dead. As they got closer, Mary got scared and screamed and as she did she started to see more of her family crawling out the floor and flying through the window. As they floated closer, Mary gave one final scream and then she fainted.

BEN MARSH (11)
Retford Oaks Academy, Retford

THE GIRL IN THE FIELD

It was then, in the field, I was hunting. I saw a girl stood in the corner of the field, I heard her singing. As I got closer it got louder and louder, until I heard nothing at all. She turned around, she had blood-red eyes, and she ran at me. She got closer and closer! The world was spinning, I could not take it. I closed my eyes and hoped for the best. I later opened them to see she was gone! The air had a misty look to it. I later found that everyone had gone missing!

STUART DAVIES (11)
Retford Oaks Academy, Retford

MALEFICENT'S CURSE

As the deep, scarlet blood leaked from her manicured finger, Aurora felt aggression and anger build through her body. Her fists clenched with fury and she felt a strange sensation taking over her soul, a strange sensation that she couldn't control. Aurora then caught a glimpse of a sharp, shiny knife glistening in the summer's sun! She grabbed it, clutching it tight, then, without hesitation, she ran towards her father! Aurora plunged the knife through her father's heart...
She is the devil, with a passion to kill and right now she is making an eerie grin, staring right at you!

ROBYN DARLINGTON (12)
Retford Oaks Academy, Retford

THE ZOMBIE APOCALYPSE

It was a dark unsuspecting night when a man called Jeff glanced out of the window. There were at least twenty-one people outside walking with a limp and drenched in blood. Suddenly, there was a massive *bang*. Downstairs, Jeff ran as fast as he could down the creaky staircase with a baseball bat. *Bang, bang,* the zombies were gone with a thwack round the head by the bat. He walked down the street which was deserted. He entered a house, there was a woman shivering. They were the only two people in the helpless country. Will they survive?...

DANIEL HORNAGOLD (12)
Retford Oaks Academy, Retford

UNTITLED

Breathing shallow, my heart racing, my ice-cold feet stumbling through the forest. I trip over my untied laces. Wailing out in pain as I crumble to the ground. Frozen leaves crunch beneath my weight, sweat drips from my face. Picking myself up I check my grazed hand, wiping my forehead in the process I find blood on my hand but no sweat. I feel dizzy at this point and my eyes are blurred. I rub them with my sore fingers. I can almost make out the shadow in the darkness. He's after me...

MEGAN HOWE (14)
Retford Oaks Academy, Retford

RED RIDING HOOD – WOLF EXTINCTION

When I was little I met a wolf. Since then wolf extinction began. Me and my grandma have been hunting wolves since that day. We're hunting the alpha which, when we kill, will stop all of this. I've killed 1001 wolves so far.

Today something happened, the moon turned red, the alpha was here. So we set out after it, then something unusual happened. They were all there, the wolves. And there he was, the alpha. My grandma said, 'Go,' so she dealt with them as I jumped. My axe smashed his skull. He was dead.

JOSH SMITH (12)
Retford Oaks Academy, Retford

THE WICKED FAIRY GODMOTHER

There was a girl named Cinderella, she lived with her wicked stepsisters. One day they were invited to a ball at the palace but Cinderella was not allowed. Cinderella had to stay at home and clean. They went to the ball, leaving Cinderella alone. Cinderella felt incredibly sad and began to cry. Suddenly, a fairy godmother appeared and whispered, 'I'll send you to the ball!'

All was well, until midnight. The fairy godmother saw how much fun she was having and magicked her away to a damp cell. That's where she stayed for the rest of her life.

EMILY MARFLEET (11)
Retford Oaks Academy, Retford

THE BEAST

I was panting, my heart beating fast. My father has been kidnapped and I want to know where he is. A twig snapped. 'Belle,' I heard a deep, husky voice say behind me; too frightened to turn around. I heard a swift move, the moonlight shone down to reveal a hairy, monstrous beast, blood dripping down his deadly fangs. I was too petrified to move. It growled, a deep, threatening growl. I tried to remain calm, not wanting it to think I was scared. It stepped towards me, I stepped back. Suddenly, it lunged at me and everything went black.

KATIE NGUYEN (12)
Retford Oaks Academy, Retford

TRIPUNZLE

Once upon a time, in 1985, there was a beautiful princess but she was being held hostage in a skyscraper by terrorists. One day a young prince thought he could save her. One day he told the princess to collect rope then left.
In three months time he returned and the princess had collected enough rope to stretch down to the ground from the top, so the prince yelled, 'Rapunzel, Rapunzel, let down your rope.' So, she let down her rope and the prince started to climb up it but when he was half way up, it snapped.

DANIEL NEWBITT (12)
Retford Oaks Academy, Retford

THE BEAST OF LEVERTON

Last night, I was walking home. I heard a low growl coming from behind me. I looked but nothing was there. I heard it again. Then I saw the beast of Leverton. It had long fangs, dripping with blood. It looked very hungry. It looked like I was his next meal. I was nervous, my heart was pounding, my stomach flipped. The beast was ready to pounce. In that split second, the beast pounced. It tried to rip me to pieces but all it got was my right arm. I managed to escape. I ran as fast as I could!

LUCY WILKINSON (12)
Retford Oaks Academy, Retford

POCAHONTAS

A loud bang came from behind the withered group of trees and bushes. She had hoped it was some form of entertainment that would take up the rest of her day. The young girl was disappointed and intrigued when she found not entertainment but a band of brutish big men that carried round huge pieces of wood creating a huge wall. One of them seemed to stand out. He was beautiful. Suddenly, an arrow shot out of the trees and took down one of the big men. They took down everyone with bloodshed. She realised it was her people. Savages.

SAMMIE BABU (11)
Retford Oaks Academy, Retford

THE BIG BAD SLEEPOVER

Toby was having a sleepover with Harry. They were both excited.
At 11pm they got bored so they went off into the forest. They got
to the forest and started playing a game of tag, until... they heard
a long, abnormal 'Grrooooann.' Then they heard footsteps slowly
coming towards them. Then silence... *Zoom,* a disorientated figure
appeared... Zombie! They were petrified and screamed but then
sensed it was upset. They went towards it. Toby's dad saw them and
screamed, 'Get away from it!' It was too late, the zombie grabbed
Toby and ran... Where are they? We'll never know.

JONATHAN HORNAGOLD (12)
Retford Oaks Academy, Retford

LEFT ALONE

Steve stumbled across the desert land. He was left to die by his
not loyal team of marine soldiers. The pains from a shot wound
were agonising. He was finding it hard to stand on his own two feet.
Eventually, he had to take off his heavy, worn-out armour. Steve
was then confronted by a sand dune, which towered over him like a
god. Plodding his way up the sand dune, he quickly fell down again.
Exhausted. That's what he was. He knew this was it. The end of his
time. He lay down and painfully let himself die.

ZADE ALKHABAZ (11)
Rushcliffe School, Nottingham

Rapunzel

Grow, grow, grow, it's all it ever does! I have to keep it. It's weird, for me every time I sing it grows! Is it weird? Am I weird? It's my birthday coming up. I'm gonna ask my mother if I can just go touch grass, swoop my golden hair all around! Leave this stupid tower! Oh here she comes. I can do it, I can ask her! 'Mother, can I leave the tower?' Then suddenly she goes furious. Then seconds later I'm saying, 'Sorry.' I just let down my hair and she left. Unexpectedly, *bang!* There was a man!

Alisha Humphries (11)
Rushcliffe School, Nottingham

Remix Of Three Little Pigs

What is this... Yesterday everyone was going about living their normal lives, but today... Well, as I looked out my window all I can see is devastation, cars halfway through exploding, like time has frozen. There is no one in the city, I knew the world had secrets but... seriously. Wait, what's that in the distance? I can't quite make out what it is, it's getting closer. I see blood, horror and anger in its eyes... It's... it's... a pig? I can see its pain, a wolf killed its family, its home and it destroyed everything in sight.

Aaron Taylor (12)
Rushcliffe School, Nottingham

THE GUITAR

Once upon a time, there lived a boy who carried and played a guitar everywhere he went. People loved the music as it made them happy. One day a bully heard the music and became jealous so he took the guitar so he could play it for himself. But every time he did, the guitar sounded like it was crying. After many days of trying he threw the guitar into a shed. Every day when the bully was away the guitar would play itself. It hoped the boy would hear its melody. To this day it still waits...

KABIR AWAN (12)
Rushcliffe School, Nottingham

DEVIL DRIVER

One day there was a girl called Megan, who was playing with her friend, Olivia. They were playing Frisbee when it flew onto the road, so Megan ran out on the road. She saw a truck driver with no eyes, and slobber dripping from its mouth. So she shouted, 'Help, Olivia!' So she ran out onto the curb. When the van hit Megan her leg got broken and blood was oozing out of her leg. Olivia took her jacket off and wrapped it around her leg to stop the blood but unfortunately Megan passed away.

ALFIE CUMBERLAND (12)
Rushcliffe School, Nottingham

THE TALES OF SIR WOLFINGTON 21ST

My name is Sir Wolfington 21st and I am inside Big Bad Riding Shoe's belly. Here's how it all started... My granddad, Sir Wolfington 19th, wanted me to get rid of the horrible bread in the pit of Sparta because it tasted absolutely horrible so I did. I was on my way back to his mansion when Big Bad Riding Shoe jumped at me and so I challenged her to a fight, resulting in her eating me whole. Of course, I tried to get out by threatening to kick her into the pit of Sparta but it was no use.

ZAK MCCONNOCHIE (12)
Rushcliffe School, Nottingham

LIGHT

Zak stood in his bedroom surrounded by Lego, books and comics. It was late at night when he saw the first signs; the bulb blew and smothered him in a blanket of darkness. Something smashed, he assumed it was the window as it seemed to shatter on its way to the floor. Then came the footprints, four of them. Glimmering, a figure stood at the door. The street lamps darkened as Zak watched through what was left of his window. 'I've collected the light!' exclaimed the figure fiercely. In a flash the figure disappeared...

JOE EVERITT (12)
Rushcliffe School, Nottingham

I'M CHUCK

If I lied to the queen, would it be that bad? Right now I'm taking Snow White to the forest where I have to kill her. I'm Chuck, by the way, the queen's personal assistant. More like slave. I can't kill Snow, I love her. But, if I don't kill her I either have to lie to the queen or prepare to get my head chopped off! Wait, I could stay in the forest! I could run away with Snow White and just not go back, that's what I'll do. Why didn't I think of that before?

ELLA PROBERT (11)
Rushcliffe School, Nottingham

DEATH

'Argh!' I screamed in pain. I woke in the night, staring at the stars in the sky and the towering trees. Where was I? I heard a loud but short bang. I then realised I was in a stream. I got up with pain everywhere. I finally got up to find myself in a forest with massive oak trees. Just then, I heard branches snapping, leaves crunching... and the sounds were getting closer to me. Somebody was near. A dark, tall figure appeared. 'Where am I?' I questioned in a soft, scared voice. 'You're in the Hunger Games,' they said.

LEWIS MOSSABERI (11)
Rushcliffe School, Nottingham

THE BOY WITH NO NAME

Once upon a time there was a boy, he lived in a normal village with a normal family. When he was born, his parents never gave him a name! He never went to school and never had friends. One day, when they were driving back from the supermarket, there was a *crash!* It was like seeing a car full of blood. No one survived! Now every time a family drive past that road where he died he follows you and haunts you forever! You never know, he might be staring at you right now, outside your window! Watch out!

MADDIE BEESLEY (12)
Rushcliffe School, Nottingham

THE NOTE

I open the door into my house. 'Hello, Mum, I'm home.' There's no reply. The only noise I can hear is a repetitive tick-tock of the clock sat on the wall. A soft jingle comes from upstairs; I recognise it as my music box's gentle tune. I follow the noise upstairs into my room, but nobody is to be seen. My room's a mess. Everything turned upside down and out of its place. A note is stuck to the back of my door: 'You are in danger'. A million questions fly around my head but there's only one solution. Run...

KRIPA KAPHLE (12)
Rushcliffe School, Nottingham

TAIL

The fresh smell of pork filled my clogged nostrils. It was here. I slowly peered round my hiding spot to see a scrumptious pig trot its way to the decaying house, in a hurry as if it was afraid. It should be afraid. I was here. I realised I would take a different route into the melancholy house of pure terror. How could a pig live in such conditions? I climbed to the top of the house and jumped into the chimney to see a pot of boiling water. That was the end of my tail!

CALLUM ARMSTRONG (12)
Rushcliffe School, Nottingham

THE WATCHING

As she walked through the dark, gloomy forest, *crunch* as she went through the unscathed forest. As she walked eyes were watching her. Her breathing hardened. *Bang!* The eyes ran with her as she got to the house. She ran faster, *snap!* The jaws swallowed her in one go, she struggled to get air as she broke the teeth of the beast. She went flying to the floor. She stabbed the beast. The beast died with a howl as the corpse hit the floor. As the rotting started, she ran home with her blood-soaked cape and her hood, red!

RYAN PORTASS (12)
Rushcliffe School, Nottingham

LIFELESS SHE WAS

Lifeless she was. I almost felt guilty seeing her lie there motionless. Her heart was no longer beating. My job was done; she was dead. The bitten apple dropped from her cold, purple hands. As I turned my back to her body and stepped away, I felt a shiver run down my spine. I couldn't go back now. She was already dead. Now I could finally be the best. The prettiest. The queen. I shall be the fairest of all the lands. Nobody shall question me anymore, they won't dare. For their sake, let's hope they don't try to.

MADISON WRIGHT (12)
Rushcliffe School, Nottingham

ASYLUM

I lay in bed, traumatised by my dream. What if it actually happened? Hesitantly I walked to the window and opened the curtain. I froze in horror. It was in fact not a dream, but reality. There were bodies everywhere. Men, women, children. Then I saw one body in particular. Mine. My heart must have skipped a beat. I fell to the floor. Someone must have found me because I woke up in an asylum full of bloodthirsty criminals. They all stared at me with their menacing eyes. I was the weak one. It was time to say goodbye life!

AIMEE LLOYD (12)
Rushcliffe School, Nottingham

UNTITLED

I've got to run faster, faster, like a wild animal running away from stronger and bigger ones. *Bang*, I heard. Was that an explosion? I think it was. That noise was really close, maybe I should check it out. *Bang*, I heard again, it made me jump but this time it was a gunshot. I kept on running, I found a broken old house. It looked creepy. I had to stay in there until it stopped raining, it was like God hated me. I went inside and saw a big hole in the middle of the floor. *Bang!*

DEANDRE KNOWLES (12)
Rushcliffe School, Nottingham

LITTLE RED RIDING HOOD

My heart was throbbing, I had ripped my red cape on a bramble when I was being chased. Being chased by the huge wolf. I was only supposed to be taking cookies to my grandma when a huge wolf started to chase me. It probably wanted the cookies. In the distance, I could see the huge wolf tiptoeing towards me. I had to get to Grandma's house, it was only a few metres away, but could I get there without being seen by the huge wolf?

ROBBIE ASHER (12)
Rushcliffe School, Nottingham

THE SCENT

The wind echoed the screams of his last victim. The blood dripped from his mouth, quenching his urge for more red liquid. He strode across the deserted forest, watching carefully for his next target. Caught through his senses was the fresh smell of frightened meat. He charged towards the mouth-watering aroma, thoughtless of what lay around. The scent led to a poorly built straw house. Without a second thought, the hazardous hunter knocked onto the unstable door. Taking a luxurious inhale of what lay behind the flimsy door, the predator cunningly said, 'Little pig, little pig, let me come in.'

HANA KALEEM (13)
Rushcliffe School, Nottingham

SMASHED

The commotion outside was unbearable, the screeching of eager women filled the autumn air. The prince attempted to calm the women who, already had produced multiple scratches along his delicate face. Some women held solid wooden clubs and large logs, ready to shatter the glass shoe into a thousand small pieces. The wild women scrambled for the shoe, pouncing like panthers through the undergrowth. A flash of silver swooped past the prince's face. The world stopped, the women fell silent, the shoe was smashed, but so was the prince. Suddenly, the air was filled with cheering. They were both gone.

NIAMH GATER (12)
Rushcliffe School, Nottingham

THE RED-HOODED GIRL

She looked so tempting standing there, seemingly her red cloak mirrored the colour of her blood. He needed the right moment to pounce upon his prey. Her scent was a tingling sensation that tickled his wet and damp nose. Thankfully, she didn't scream, unlike his other victims but all he could think about was her blood trickling into his mouth.

SAVERA IQBAL (13)
Rushcliffe School, Nottingham

THE SHATTERED QUEEN

Once upon a time, in the depths of winter, the flakes of snow were falling like feathers from clouds. A majestic queen sat on her throne and gazed at her reflection, in awe of her beauty. Dark ebony hair, white snow, blood lips. Anger, confusion, hatred ran through her mind as she saw the face of her new enemy. The girl had a complexion as clear as a noon day, more beautiful than the queen. The girl locked the queen's gaze in the mirror, red eyes, they shattered the glistening mirror and shattered the queen's life. The girl had revenge...

TRUDI ANDREW (12)
Rushcliffe School, Nottingham

SEVEN IN THE MORNING

As I tried my best to remove the paranormal creature's claw from my impaled chest, I glanced over at my alarm clock. 'Seven o'clock' it read. The pain of the fiend's screech in my burning ears was nearly as painful as the claw that was previously driven into my blood-soaked chest. What could possibly be going on at seven in the morning? I began to feel faint, and realised I was about to die. Then I woke up, looked over at my clock which read 'six fifty-nine'. Then... I heard my door lock, lights flicker, and cupboard open.

GEORGE HEWITT (13)
Rushcliffe School, Nottingham

ESCAPE

She ran through the woods and didn't look back. Her dress started tearing and her make-up ran down her face. She ripped the tiara out of her hair and the necklace was pulled from her neck. She stopped and looked back at the beautiful palace she had left behind. She burst into tears and sat down in front of the deep, blue lake. All was quiet, not a person to be seen. Not an animal to be heard. She was all alone. She took a glance in the deep blue water, to find a young, beautiful, free woman.

NATASHA MARSHALL (13)
Rushcliffe School, Nottingham

MISSING

Once upon a time an ordinary, joyful little girl named Daisy lived with her mum and dad and attended the local school. Every day when she walked home from school she waved to an old man who always sat mysteriously outside his normal but slightly creepy house. Until one stormy, cold, dark winter's evening when the wind was howling and lightning could be seen, thunder could be heard, she walked past the house. The old frail man was stood by the window. He beckoned her in out of the cold. In she went. *Bang! Bang!* Never seen again...

HANNAH DAYNES (13)
Rushcliffe School, Nottingham

WORDS DON'T LIE

The words on the fragment of the ripped note taunted her, 'We don't want to go to Arybella's party... let's meet somewhere else... she's not our friend...' Arybella's heart sank. Sobbing, she threw the crumpled sheet back in the bin where she'd found it.
Minutes earlier, three excited girls had passed a note around the classroom, trying desperately to keep their secret safe. 'We don't want to go to Arybella's party late, so let's meet somewhere else first to plan the surprise. She's not our friend, she's our best friend and we have to do something really special for her'.

JESSICA DAHILL-ALLEN (12)
Rushcliffe School, Nottingham

Target Acquired

As the lone sniper lay motionless on the top of the hill, his eyes scanned the village like an eagle looking for his prey. He was looking for the one criminal who had been escaping through the grasp of the bureau's hand for years, but now he had a chance to end their torment forever. All of a sudden, he saw him, one scar going down the side of his face. Taking his hand off the trigger, he tapped on his radio, 'I think I've got him.'
'Confirm it!'
Narrowing down the scope he got him! 'Target acquired!'

Daniel Hunter (13)
Rushcliffe School, Nottingham

Falling

Above the clouds oxygen was scarce and each breath was becoming an immense struggle. Breathlessly, Jack looked out at the deep blue sky and then down towards the whiteness below. The gargantuan stem of plant life ominously swayed under his feet, nausea bubbling up in his stomach. A miniscule patch of cloud had broken away from the vast sheet, a small enough gap for Jack to feel faint, seeing his small house one thousand miles beneath him. All of his throbbing blood rushed to his skull as blue faded to black and a green blur flew by his ear.

Guy McEwan
Rushcliffe School, Nottingham

THE TRIBAL WARRIOR

He crept through the thorny bush. His target was sighted, the image was in his head; An elk, so vulnerable, so weak. His concentration focused, ready to strike, ready to hunt. An autumn winter breeze flew by his irony wavy hair. His heart racing, he picked up his old wooden bow. His sweaty hands gripped the wood. He picked up a birch arrow ready to take the shot. His hand pulled back the fragile string, he pulled it. The arrow flew like a bullet from a firing gun heading towards the elk. It was dead, it lay still, no movement.

TOM LEDGER (13)
Rushcliffe School, Nottingham

LIFE MEANS DEATH

I pounced; the whole forest fell silent as a blood-curdling scream emerged from the pig's mouth. How much he yearned for the end of his life, how much he yearned for his brothers to help him. The forest fell silent. I felt like being a nuisance by deciding how I should kill my prey. He vigorously squirmed for his escape. I prolonged his life for hours and hours, giving him a slight glimmer of hope that he might survive. For hours and hours I held him there. I struck the final blow, there was a blood-curdling scream.

ROHAN BERI (12)
Rushcliffe School, Nottingham

DRAGONREND

Quietly I opened my eyes and stared into the darkness of the sky haven temple. There was that curious thrumming, that silent chorus which I could hear by virtue of the dragon's blood that ran through my veins, blood that I had known only existed until Whiterun, until that stormy day when lightning carved up the sky along with cruel talons and a dragon, it fell by my combined might of arrows and swords. The killing blow was mine. That is the only thing I know of my shrouded past, now it's for the future, the douvahkiin, the dragonborn!

MAX WHITCHURCH (12)
Rushcliffe School, Nottingham

TO BECOME THE FAIREST OF THEM ALL

The blood-covered knife lay beside my elegant orange dress that was spread out on the lush green grass like a rose in bloom. I forced a grin onto my delicate and impeccable face. I had finally done the deed. Nothing could stop me now. Snow White's lifeless body lay in front of me. A river of dark red blood escaped her pale blue dress in the middle of her stomach. Her eyes were motionless. Her skin as pale and as cold as ice. Finally, after sixteen long and tiring years, I was the fairest of them all.

GINNY HARRIS (12)
Rushcliffe School, Nottingham

THE LITTLE MERMAID'S BIGGEST MISTAKE

It was love at first sight. He was drowning in the crystal-clear sea with no one to save him. What else could I do but help him? I swam to him and pulled him to the surface, then I took him to the beautiful sandy beach by the palace. All he had was his ripped clothes and a revolver. I should have known! Humans can never be trusted! Before I knew it he started breathing. Then he opened his emerald eyes. He grabbed his loaded pistol! *Bang!* Bullet straight through my heart. Why had I trusted that stupid human...

JOANNE ELLIS (12)
Rushcliffe School, Nottingham

LIFE OF AN OWL

I just sat there. On my bench. All day and night. Nothing good had ever happened to me, until now. I was staring at the small, thin path below me, trying to spot something, anything, and I was in luck as a young girl skipped past. She wore some ragged white clothes and a stunning bright red cape with a nice little hood. She just skipped along, with her cape and a small basket, oblivious to me. I'm a very noticeable brown owl thank you very much. Maybe I should wear a red cape with a little red hood too.

JAMIE STUART ALEXANDER BARKER (11)
Rushcliffe School, Nottingham

Big Bad Grandma

Once upon a time an ugly, hairy wolf wandered around in the woods when suddenly he recognised, a young small girl dressed in red. The wolf had seen her before visiting her frail grandma. All of a sudden a thought came to his mind. He was starving so why not give Grandma a delicious visit.

The wooden door creaked open and from the corner of his hairy eye he spotted snoring Grandma. The wolf silently crept up on her. Without warning the grandma rapidly jumped on the startled wolf. She viciously bit him. Her eyes were red... A vampire!

Vinaya Patel (13)
Rushey Mead Secondary School, Leicester

Humans Are Animals Too

The words played along my lips as they fumbled with abhorrence, like numb, tired fingers reaching for the strings - reaching for the chords of release. It clutches the only warmth within their sombre walls but it has long since leached into the algid air. Its heart weakens as we press our selfish noses against the glass, the glass that retains life. Don't you ever feel overcome with pure guilt because I do, but no - we are told that they are lesser beings. They are animals.

Sophiya Sian (12)
Rushey Mead Secondary School, Leicester

LONDON MINOTAUR

The geophysics was right, there was a large cavern under St James' Park, London. The archaeologists gathered around as the last pieces of dirt were lifted. The cavern was revealed, air flew in. The light met the walls, and a large creature was shown. As the air and light hit the beast, it stirred and the creature brayed; what was one Minotaur were now thousands coming out of the maze surrounding the cavern. Creatures climbed the gorge then flew to the top of Buckingham Palace, that's when the destruction began. This was the end of humanity and civilisation forever.

TOM JAMES HARRINGTON
St Crispin's School, Leicester

FARM BOY

All I can see are the flames rising between my eyes but all I could think of is I've escaped, I'm finally free. My feet are burning but as I step away it gets better. I fall to the ground, everything starts to get darker, I can see no more. Then I start to think *why give up now? Why let go?* There is no point of stopping. I can hear footsteps. The more I wait the louder it gets. I guess I don't belong in this world. I guess it's time to go. I am only a farm boy.

FAROUK BARAKAT (12)
St Peter's Independent School, Northampton

THE TWIST BETWEEN THE THREE

A loud howl tumbled antagonistically along the path through the woods. Jack and Cinderella looked at each other as the silence afterwards deafened them. They ran through the winding trees to meet the wolf attacking Little Red (as though it seemed.) Red and Black flashed wildly as Cinderella and Jack stood there motionlessly, somehow they couldn't move. After the final screech everything fell silent, still and lifeless. Blood was spilt everywhere and Little Red stood, proud to not have lost a single drop of human blood. The storm awoke but the wolf was put in a sleep that was eternal!

JENNIFER SHIN (12)
St Peter's Independent School, Northampton

SWIPE OF A DAGGER

She stood there in the dark mist, her eyes white and riddled with maggots in the moonlight. Her dress was ragged, dirty, her eyes sunken, she had a wide bloody smile. Holding a dagger in one hand and reaching out with the other she walked closer, humming the deadly tune of ring-a-ring o' roses. Her dirty matted hair swaying as she came closer. She walked with a limp. She was now face to face with me. I knew I was about to die, then it was black. I was dead... At the hands of my little baby sister.

NELL LOPEZ WOODWARD (12)
St Peter's Independent School, Northampton

SEVEN LITTLE GOATS AND THE WOLF

There is no way to resist hunger. That's why Mother Goat had to visit the supermarket. 'Yes, Mum, we'll behave,' said the goats. In fact they knew about Wolf's plan to attack their house. They armed themselves in sticks and logs and they waited.
At midnight the wolf came. He was quickly knocked out and tied up. When Mother Goat came home she noticed a pie. She ate it and asked her kids, 'Where did you get the meat from, children?' 'Well, it's our little secret!' the kiddie goats replied with a grim, suspicious smile on their hairy faces.

JAKUB JAN SWITALSKI (12)
St Peter's Independent School, Northampton

UNTITLED

They tore out chunks of me! I couldn't take it anymore, my candy canes were snapped off, my fruit pastels were in their digestive systems and my gingerbread men lost their perfectly round heads! I was about to demolish them there and then when suddenly, a ratty old lady came out of my sticky liquorice door. She led Hansel and Gretel in as she acted all sweet and innocent, only to try and kill them later. She got mad at them and told them off - and that's when she said the wrong words, 'My house,' so I killed them!

ALEXIA PANAYIS (13)
St Peter's Independent School, Northampton

WOLF OF THE MOON

The wind blew wildly as the fading sun retreated. The sea raged and the grass swayed angrily in the wind. On the hill, the graveyard remained, as the sky grew black and Kara changed. Kara was dressed in dirty rags just covering her body. Her straggly hair hung under her bony chin. She growled at the crooked church, snarling till her teeth ached. *Splash,* the water lapped the sands of Wolf Beach. A beam of magical light arose from the sky, hitting her trembling bones. Wild hair ripped through her rags and horns rose from her head. Who was she?

NATASHA ARDEN (11)
The Bramcote School, Nottingham

THE GRIM DAYS

First David disappeared, then Bob, James, Danny, Cregan, Rodrigo, Roden, Zach, Oliver and Keith. Each day, someone disappeared. When Lucas went to the victims' houses, he saw on the wall, in blood - *Guess Who?* As if they wanted you to guess who was going to be next. All the adults fled, leaving the kids alone, apart from one adult, Mr Jackson. Little did they know he was the reason they were disappearing. Then Lucas' friends Penny, Charlie and Ben were found dead, stuffed into Ben's closet. Mr Jackson was revealed as the killer and fled, never to be seen...

OWEN MURRAY (11)
The Bramcote School, Nottingham

THE ROOM

The room was a small place but with many uncovered passages. The inside had mouldy wooden chairs and tables with cuts in them. Blood splatters everywhere. A single curtain moving, but there were no windows. They were boarded up so the children couldn't see the horror. The room was a place that invoked nightmares. No one went in, apart from a thirteen-year-old boy, he wanted to go in. He didn't tell anyone though, he knew they would blab. He opened the door so it creaked, he went in. But did he ever come out? Did he know?

AMY NICOLE CROWTHER (13)
The Bramcote School, Nottingham

THE MAN IN THE SNOW

Blake was flipping through channels on his TV when he heard part of a report of a murderer on the loose. After locking his doors and windows, he looked out of the sliding door in the kitchen. At first he saw nothing, but he quickly noticed a dark figure in the back garden, getting closer, a grotesque smile spreading on his face. Blake fumbled with his phone, until he realised, no footprints appeared in the snow behind the figure. The man in his garden was a reflection!

ISOBEL MILLER (12)
The Bramcote School, Nottingham

IS MY MUM AN ALIEN?

As usual, me and my friends were playing football. Time had passed and I walked home. As soon as I got there, Mum was on the couch, normally she would call me and tell me to set the table or something. Instead, she lay there, eating a chocolate bar, but her face was covered in a sort of sticky stuff. Was she an alien?
For the rest of the day I stayed in my room, horrified. Mum called me down for lunch, but her face was clean. Was it just a mask?

HALIMA MAHMOOD (12)
The Bramcote School, Nottingham

WALLACE AND THE WEDDING

Once, there was a girl called Layla who had a pet monster called Wallace. Today was the day of her brother Henry's wedding. The wedding started all going well, until the small monster came!
Screams came from the guests as Wallace came forward. He was heading for Layla. Henry ran for the monster with his sword.
'No that's Wallace,' screamed Layla.
'He's a monster, not a friend,' Henry yelled back. Wallace ran and hid under Layla.
'What are you doing here?' Layla asked.
'I'm hungry,' Wallace replied. With that he ate the mother of the bride and the bride himself.

ALICE THOMPSON
The Holgate Academy, Nottingham

WICKED AND WILEY

Wicked and Wily, a pair of wolves. Both phenomenal shape-changing creatures. They live in the wood of Alkastaria. Wily went exploring. Wicked demanded she stayed with her, but Wily was off. Wily glimpsed at Porman Castle, the home of Prince Jake of Alkastaria. Wow! She fell suddenly in love with him. Instantly, she became human. 'Hi, I love you,' she whispered.
He shouted back, confused, 'Who on earth are you?' She ran crying back to the woods. 'Never talk to a human again!' scolded Wicked. He died mysteriously. It was Wicked. Wily stayed away from the weird humans forever...

TIFFANY SHELTON
The Holgate Academy, Nottingham

THE GREEN LURK

'Get up Ruby!' Mum yelled. I got my pumpkin, make-up, Halloween kit and whizzed downstairs. 'See you all in a bit!' I yelled.
It was two hours later; Misty (my BFF) and I decided to go to the gruesome graveyard. A scary sound lurked behind us. Green smoke was hovering in the air. It suddenly flew into Misty. 'What's wrong?' I said to her. She charged at me. I ran, huffing and puffing; my life depended on it. Suddenly, she caught up with me. My screaming was extremely loud. I was caught. 'Nooooooo!'

IVY MILLER (12)
The Holgate Academy, Nottingham

HANSEL AND GRETEL – THE SECRET AGENTS

'Hello! Anybody there?' Gretel yelled at the small gingerbread house. 'I'm here for the... thing!'
'Is that Agent 111443585?' An old woman's voice spoke inside the house.
'Yes.'
'Come in.' Gretel walked in on a strong smell of poison. 'Ah, my dear. Are you here for the... recipe?' The old woman whispered mysteriously.
'Yes. Where does it lie?' Gretel wondered.
'Under the stove.'
As soon as she said that Hansel (Agent 4444444446796) shot through the door. 'Good news!' We're not going to get lost! I've been tearing paper up as breadcrumbs!' Hansel yelled joyfully. And the recipe was gone forever.

JESSICA THOMPSON (13)
The Holgate Academy, Nottingham

GRIM TALE

We were talking about myths in class. The bell went, but I was left wondering about The Shadow. It appeared every ten years to take over someone's body. Wait - wasn't it due to appear today? The clock struck twelve and my world just stopped. I was at Tesco and it happened. I lost control. It was like a stranger in my own body. Then I heard it... frantic screaming. The store seemed to be full of police, pointing their weapons at me. Suddenly, *bang*! I fell in a pool of blood, but not mine... it was black.

CHRISTY MORGAN (12)
The Holgate Academy, Nottingham

THE FAIRY TALE MURDERER

I've always thought I was a rebel. I'm not trying to confess, but I would like some credit for the work that I've done. It's me, the fairy tale murderer! Remember that Humpty dude? Did you really think he just fell off a wall? No, I pushed him. Just like I pushed Jill. I bet you also remember my mate Hansel? He's my partner in crime. We both told the witch to eat her. We're master criminals, it's what we do. Anyway, I have to go murder Baby Bear and Goldilocks now. My only ambition is to kill that wolf...

LOTTIE BAXTER (12)
The Redhill Academy, Nottingham

THE PALE WHITE LIE REVEALED

There stood the brave hunter, smiling. The job had been done. There in his hands, was a box the beautiful queen knew all too well... She had never wished to kill anyone but by doing it she was saving lives. The girl with skin as white as snow and lips as red as roses was not as sweet as she seemed. The queen knew all her secrets but was being carefully watched at all times. I knew her well; being her servant. She couldn't tell anyone! It made her crazy! No one could know and that was worst of all...

TASMIN WHITTLE (13)
The Redhill Academy, Nottingham

Hatter's Asylum

The Mad Hatter was rocking, rocking slowly backwards and forth in his chair. Staring into nothing, smiling and showing all of his teeth. The asylum was a prison to him, he knew he was never getting out. He used to dream how he got here; falling, falling slowly down a dark hole.

Every Sunday a young girl with blonde hair and a blue dress would come to visit him, you could overhear the stories she would tell him. It sounded like a load of nonsense to be honest. But despite all, he sat there rocking slowly and smiling.

Katelynn Bodycott
The Redhill Academy, Nottingham

No Way Down!

He beat me. My harp playing doesn't satisfy him any longer. The burning worry that a mischievous child breaking into our home, stealing our possessions angers him. Scares him even. He turns, clenching his fists, his bloodshot pulsating eyes. I plead. He takes no mercy. In seconds I'm bruised and broken. I'm crying now, blood pouring from my lip. A noise. His attention is drawn to it and not to me. A hand grabs the top of the beanstalk. He grabs my golden goose and bolts. Lucky thing. He can escape. My husband turns to me. I hold my breath!

Olivia Davies (13)
The Redhill Academy, Nottingham

MY CONFESSION

Sometimes people are pushed too far. To a point of no return. They try. They try so hard to carry on. But you can't accomplish the impossible. I was a slave. Nothing more. There to cook and clean for my own stepfamily. I felt trapped and when you trap an animal in a cage it will fight back. What did they expect? I look around now. Trying to force a single tear. Not for them, but for me. To prove to myself I am not that animal, but I can't. I regret nothing. I did it, I killed them!

LAURA ELIZABETH STEPHENSON (13)
The Redhill Academy, Nottingham

CINNAMON SWEAT

They had caught him. The path home was like walking to hell. Cinnamon sweat dripped down his forehead; he was getting soggy. The oven, his maker, scolded him, glaring at him. He should never have run. He'd gloated too; that couldn't have helped. But it was too late now. His steaming punishment awaited him. Out of the cupboard came a plate. He was placed on it whilst they set up. A stool was drawn to the table. The glass was placed by him. He hoped it would be quick. The glass loomed towards him. He went under. Dunked. He crumbled.

FREYA FISHER (12)
The Redhill Academy, Nottingham

BLOODTHIRSTY

1880, a mother and child have died a vicious death from an unknown kind. I wasn't happy about the move, however, Mum said it was for the best. I didn't speak to Mum as we reached the house. I found my new room and, as I opened the door, there were three dolls sitting on my bed. I thought it was a moment where my brain was playing tricks but it wasn't. I attempted to pick one up; a sharp pain as the other grabbed my arm, the third sinking its teeth into me, screaming, hitting the floor, only silence.

TYLER SCOTHERN (13)
The Redhill Academy, Nottingham

PAY YOUR BILLS

The piggy strutted to his bro's flat, that action was craaazy! Following was that nasty hard wolf with his crew, knocking down all them houses. After piggy two had let him in we had an action-packed thriller right on his doorstep. Bricks spewed everywhere. Piggy one and two wadded with their trousers down low to piggy three's house. After hours of destruction the wolf had only come for his furniture. Piggy hadn't paid his bills recently. Piggy unfortunately got evicted from his home and now resides in the sunny town of Brighton with his lovely girlfriend Sarah, the pig!

JACK BANNISTER (13)
The Redhill Academy, Nottingham

LITTLE RED

Her crimson-red cape blew ferociously in the wind. As she strolled down the path, Little Red got out the chocolate muffins her mum had made to give to her grandma, and started gobbling them down. She skipped towards the sweet scented flowers that her mum also had told her to give to Grandma, however, she picked up the ones that had been kicked to the side and continued to walk on the path to Grandma's. Suddenly, she heard a terribly frightening scream coming from her grandma's house. Red pulled out her bow and arrow and shot at the dark silhouette.

RUQAIYAH ASGHAR (13)
The Redhill Academy, Nottingham

THE PIGS INTERVENE

Three goats lived next to a river. The eldest goat looked up from the grass and saw the lush pasture on the other side. He trotted to the bridge that spanned the river, but before his hoof touched the cobbles, a growl came from beneath. A troll lumbered up the embankment towards the goat. It opened its mighty jaws, however, no words came out. It looked towards the horizon, confused. Two pigs, followed by a wolf, ran past, knocking the troll into the fast moving water and continued towards a brick house. The goats crossed the bridge and ate.

JOEL BOND (14)
The Redhill Academy, Nottingham

You Shall Not Go To The Ball

The first tick of midnight. 'I must go!' she stammered.
'No! You must stay and have one last dance!' he exclaimed. He
dragged her across the floor and spun her, she tried to escape.
The last tick of midnight. Her hand started glowing. Then her legs.
Then her head! Her whole body started glowing! Her hair became
tangled and her dress started to rip. The light dimmed as she lay on
the ground. 'What is this? Some kind of joke? Take her to the tower!
Chop her into tiny pieces!' he shouted. There is now nothing left of
old Cindy.

KATE SIMPSON-HALLAS (13)
The Redhill Academy, Nottingham

THE BOY WHO CRIED MY NAME

I am fed up of sitting here in these woods, not eating anything. One day when that boy shouts my name, nobody will believe him. He won't be laughing when he is all mine. Every morning I wake up to him crying wolf. Today, I am feeling lucky. Yesterday his leader wouldn't let him in the garden at all. I'm hiding behind the tree waiting for him. He finally comes skipping out into the flower gardens to project his voice and cry wolf. I see the chance and run for him. *Chomp! Chomp!* Slowly I stroll back into the forest.

CURTIS KNIGHT (12)
The Redhill Academy, Nottingham

MAGICAL FAIRY TALES COMING ALIVE

Goldilocks caught a glimpse there. Three terrified pigs, alone, begging for money. A pumpkin vehicle parked up, it was the Fairy Godmother. She gave them three seeds and then fled until she was no longer seen. Goldilocks analysed carefully. The pigs planted the seeds. However, these seeds weren't any old seeds, they were magic. Afterwards, they grew into a beanstalk. Down came a rolling egg, which had a great fall. The pigs climbed up. They met a witch, who swapped a necklace for a pie. They ate it and all turned into bears. Would Goldilocks be able to rescue them?

PAVAN LANDA (13)
The Redhill Academy, Nottingham

THE SPIRITUAL TREE

There once lived a girl named Goldie and she never left her cramped cottage in the forest. However, one day she left her house to visit her poorly grandma. If she had known what would happen that day she would have never left her house. When she had left, three secretive little pigs entered the house and rummaged through the entire house looking for food. However, a giant had appeared outside the house. This was not a pleasant giant and he crushed the house until it was rubble. Goldie never returned. Why? Well, I guess we will never know.

ALEXANDRA GALLAGHER (12)
The Redhill Academy, Nottingham

Rapunzel, Rapunzel, Let Down Your Hair

The prince heard her call. A beautiful yet scared yell crossed his ears. He rode on through the shrubs on horse. At last he found it, an amazing stone tower hidden in depths of the woods and which held a beautiful princess, locked behind the bars that bolted against the stone window, at the very top. The prince opened his mouth only to say... 'Rapunzel, Rapunzel, let down your beautiful hair,' and as he clutched her soft, silky hair he began to lift, his heels to ankle, knee and up! Then it halts halfway up, suddenly he fell... *Smash!*

Maisie Cross (12)
The Redhill Academy, Nottingham

THE REVENGE OF THE GIANT

It was all peaceful, well that was until the humans came. Jack, a young boy and his dream was to kill a giant. Little did anyone know, giants were harmless and they minded their own business. Unaware to giants, humans had an ambition. That ambition was to wipe out their species clean, right down to the bone. Jack was the only one who knew how to get to the giants' lair. Jetpack! He intelligently stole a jetpack that night, flying up to the clouds he soared. Little did he know, the giants were ready and they were very hungry!

SAM TOWLE (12)
The Redhill Academy, Nottingham

THE HOODED FIGURE

'Anyone want to buy a bow?' he shouted. No one heard him. He shouted again. Still no one heard him. He started walking around. A strange, dark, hooded figure caught his eye. 'Ay, come ere,' he said. Jack neared him. 'Come closer,' he said.

Jack slowly neared him. A sharp pain hit Jack's stomach as the figure had jabbed Jack with his fists. He continued to jab Jack till he was knocked to the floor. He started to stamp and kick him until he was knocked out. Jack's vision started to blur. The last he saw was the figure run.

NED WALKER (12)
The Redhill Academy, Nottingham

THE THREE BULLIES

A little wolf sat on a rock at the side of a mountain, all alone, when three mean pigs went up to him. The pigs kept pushing him to each other and tripping him up.

Three days later the wolf thought to himself, *I've had enough of this.* So the wolf got off the rock and went to find the pigs.

Later that day when he ran into the pigs, he told them to stop bullying him and go and do something else. The pigs did so and left the wolf alone. From then onwards he lived happily ever after.

JOE CARTER (12)
The Redhill Academy, Nottingham

INTRUDER

I saw something moving on my shelf, very small, but fast. I finished eating my healthy lunch, trees, got up and quietly went over to explore. It was climbing my clock. What on earth could it be doing? It was running for the window now, towards my secret room. I stood there in silence, inquisitively. It struggled through the window and jumped down. It was talking to my goose. 'Wow, you lay golden eggs! I could use these to sell to make back the money that I bought the beans with!' He lured the goose to him and ran away.

CHLOE LEATHERLAND (12)
The Redhill Academy, Nottingham

DOWN THE RABBIT HOLE

Alice watched as the rabbit sped around the corner. Curious, she followed it. Darting around the garden, all Alice saw were flashes of white through the leaves. Suddenly, the rabbit stopped. Slowly, it turned and looked at Alice, as if judging her. Its bleak eyes looked her up and down, daring her to do something. Filled with sudden disliking for this bothersome rabbit, Alice angrily kicked it down a nearby hole...

Two months later, Alice was in the garden again. She saw a flash of white, but, the funny thing was, this time she heard the very words, 'I'm late!'

NATALIE FITTUS (13)
The Redhill Academy, Nottingham

THREE LITTLE THIEVES

Those little thieves! Taking a wolf's clothes! I'll go find their house and I'll huff and I'll puff and I'll blow their house down! But what can I do to find them? Yes, I've got it! I can sniff their awful stenches from a mile away! If only I can put across the anger I am feeling right now. Wait, I think I can hear their evil cackles in the distance! All right, I'll creep up on them! What are the two of them thinking? Straw and wood? I can't wait to see them run in fear! Ha ha!

TYLER COOK (13)
The Redhill Academy, Nottingham

BEOWULF AND THE BEAST

The dark cave, infested with spiders and rats was not the most warm welcome to a monster's abode. However, I knew I must end his constant destruction. I stumbled to the bones on which he rested and took my chance to lunge my blade at his back; blood sprayed out and coated my body as I pulled on my sword. Too late. The sword was wedged in the (now standing) beast's scarred back. His hand reached for my chest and succeeded in lifting me. I saw his rotting canines come nearer to my head, and then I saw nothing.

FINLEY MOYE (13)
The Redhill Academy, Nottingham

GRETEL AND HANSEL

The house, so beautiful, the forbidden sweets luring us to our deaths. Can't make a sound, can't give into the temptation. But Hansel does. His lips on the blood-red frosting wakes the witch. Her deafening cackle. Those claws on my waist. It's getting hotter. Too hot to touch. Where is my way out? Hansel. He is my way out. I reluctantly clutch him, and push him into the mouth of the fire. I'm so sorry. Don't look back. Just run. Suddenly, I come to a halt. The tears blur my vision, but I can still see. It is Papa.

ROMY LETTS (14)
The Redhill Academy, Nottingham

THE RABBIT HOLE

Dazed and confused she awoke but this time she wasn't greeted by a magically insane man. Instead his vibrant hat was hanging from its threads on a bare tree branch. What had happened? A once lively wonderland was now a barren wasteland. The party dishes, posh teacups and chairs were scattered around. A colourful tail swung from a branch above her head. A pocketwatch had its pieces scattered around. It was like the magic had faded.

OLIVIA SIMMONS (14)
The Redhill Academy, Nottingham

YOUNG WRITERS INFORMATION

We hope you have enjoyed reading this book – and
that you will continue to in the coming years.

If you're a young writer who enjoys reading and creative writing, or
the parent of an enthusiastic poet or story writer, do visit our website
www.youngwriters.co.uk. Here you will find free
competitions, workshops and games, as well as
recommended reads, a poetry glossary and our blog.

If you would like to order further copies of this book, or any of
our other titles give us a call or visit **www.youngwriters.co.uk**.

Young Writers
Remus House
Coltsfoot Drive
Peterborough
PE2 9BF

(01733) 890066 / 898110
info@youngwriters.co.uk